Marcella

Marcella

OMEGA
COTTONWOOD
PRESS
Omaha, NE

MARILYN COFFEY

Originally published in 1973 by Charterhouse

ISBN-13: 978-0-9626317-4-0
Library of Congress Control Number: 2012916035
Cataloging in Publication Data on file with publisher.

Omega Cottonwood Press
13518 L St.
Omaha, NE 68137

Production, Distribution and Marketing: Concierge Marketing Inc.
www.ConciergeMarketing.com

Printed in the United States
10 9 8 7 6 5 4 3 2 1

To Arthur, who helped me find her
To Kate Yarrow, who helped me write her

*"Who is this, rising like the Nile,
like rivers whose waters surge?"*

part
one

1

The Broder twins crossed the intersection at a dead run. Sixth grade out early. Marcella should be home first, unless she dawdled, as she was inclined to do.

Mrs. Colby paused by the dining room window, parting the dimity curtains for a better view. Not that she could see much. The tangle of hedges on the far corner hid the side street so effectively that Mrs. Colby, reviewing the daily parade, often heard voices or footsteps before she actually spotted children, drifting out of the greenery like so many mirages, little more than hedge-high themselves.

Now what is this! Exasperated, Mrs. Colby pulled her handkerchief from the pocket of her seersucker housedress and spit delicately into one corner of it. She began to rub the windowpane furiously, the exertion wobbling her marcelled curls. Grease marks! How many times told them not to lean their foreheads against the window, skin grease so impossible to remove, undoubtedly have to enlist the Windex now. Rubbing, rubbing, until a clatter of voices drew her eyes back to the intersection.

But it was only Karen Harding and her clique: Donna Snow, and Linda, the principal's daughter, and Carole. Niece of the librarian, Carole. Nice girl. They all were sixth graders like Marcella, skimming out past the hedges and across the dusty street, talking, all tidy and trim in print dresses and hair bows, oxfords carefully polished, socks folded neatly over like hems. No sign of Marcella. Although, gracious knows, she could walk home with these girls every day, Karen lives only a few doors down, it would be easy enough, like Lucille, walking home with the nice fourth graders.

Mrs. Colby watched the group pass her window, so intent on their taffeta hair bows and starched dresses that she didn't sight her daughter until Marcella was halfway across the intersection, scampering along with—sure enough, wouldn't you know it, after all the times she's been spoken to—with that little Riker snip again. Might as well talk to the wind as to Marcella. Cheryl Riker, terrible child, stringy hair and a morose face, her nose always running. Poor mother a Catholic. At least Marcella looks respectable, dark hair bobbed like the other girls. A sweet face, everybody says so. Especially when she smiles. Not as pretty as Lucille, though. Mouth too big. Like her father's...but what is this? Marcella's dress hanging halfway to the ground? Merciful heavens! Must have ripped her skirt loose on the playground. Impossible, trying to keep her tidy—socks always smudging, sashes coming untied, pockets ripping off, hems coming out, hems hanging, but never whole skirts dangling! Mrs. Colby squinted through the glass.

Marcella was hidden from view behind a bush, Cheryl Riker peering through the branches, her face contorted in a grin— standing guard? But surely Cheryl couldn't see anyone in the house, it daylight and no lights on.

A flash of...cloth? A dress? Mrs. Colby was certain she'd seen it. Could it be? Marcella, in the bushes, stripping off her clothes?

Mrs. Colby waited until the girls emerged—Marcella still dressed, thank the Lord for that, but all disheveled, hair flying every which way, dress askew, caught up in back so her undergarments showed. Well, at least she fixed her skirt. After a fashion. Probably tucked it up under her sash, thinking nobody would notice.

The girls headed toward the house. Mrs. Colby let the curtain drop when she heard footsteps on the front porch. The door slammed. Giggles moved toward the stairs.

"Hello," Mrs. Colby called. "How was school?"

The girls paused, uncertain long enough for her to enter the living room.

"Okay."

"How did you rip your skirt?"

"I didn't rip it," glancing surreptitiously at Cheryl.

"What was that hanging down around your ankles, then?"

The girls eyed each other. "You'd better show her, Marcella," Cheryl said, drawing herself up and smiling at Mrs. Colby.

Marcella opened her three-ring notebook. A mass of silky cloth lay heaped on the page. Mrs. Colby recognized a slip: the fine lace, the open stitching, the narrow ribbon straps. But it was filthy—mottled with greasy red streaks.

"What could you be thinking of, Marcella, bringing home a dirty thing like that. Probably contaminated. You weren't wearing it, were you?"

Marcella ignored her question. "We think it's silk, real silk, don't we, Cheryl? It's ever so soft…"

"Nonsense," said Mrs. Colby, reaching for it. "This is only cheap rayon. Silk goes to the salvage, anyway. What were you thinking of, bringing this home?"

"And the dirt," Marcella continued doggedly, "isn't really dirt, mother, it's only lipstick. That will wash right out, won't it, Cheryl?" But Cheryl wasn't commenting. "We can keep it, can't we?"

"Lipstick?"

So it was, red streaks violating the shimmering material in strokes so bold they seemed almost purposeful, a strange calligraphy. Letters. Mrs. Colby shook the slip out, holding it gingerly by its ribbon straps. Its scalloped hem dropped. FUCK YOU, the letters said. KISS MY PRICK. Mrs. Colby hastily smashed the thing back into a wad. "Marcella! How could you? Whatever was on your mind—"

"I *told* her not to bring it home," Cheryl spoke up. "I said you wouldn't like it, with all those dirty words on it."

"But we could wash it out—"

"Where on earth did you find this filthy thing?"

Marcella, trapped, worked her jaws to check her tears.

"I found it in the bathroom."

"In the bathroom?"

"At school. In the girls' room. After gym."

"What was it doing there? You mean you took someone's slip out of the bathroom?"

"No, no! It's okay. She didn't want it anymore."

"She? Who? Who didn't want it? You mean someone gave—"

"In the *wastebasket.*" The word was blurted out harshly. "It was in the wastebasket."

Mrs. Colby erupted. "Marcella! How could you take such a disgusting...out of the *wastebasket!* Piece of trash...in the bathroom...somebody's *underwear*...who knows what has *touched* it, what kind of bacteria on it...and actually *wearing* it home, don't say you didn't, I saw you coming down the street, that slip hanging to your ankles..." Her speech faltered as she began to envision her daughter, emblazoned in the grotesque red and white garment, teetering her way home along the curbstone, all eight blocks, past the Robinsons', the Gunthers', he the county attorney, and who driving by? Or what if old Mrs. Chandler saw her, always on her porch watching...

Marcella clattered up the stairs, hair bow bouncing on her head, leaving Mrs. Colby and Cheryl staring at each other, the room still heaving, heavy as water.

"I *told* her you wouldn't like it if she—" Cheryl began.

"You'd better go now." That Cheryl clearly insolent. No manners at all. And Lucille, only ten, too young for this, might be walking in the door any minute. No need to expose her. Mrs. Colby tried to stem her heavy breathing.

Cheryl shrugged. She was used to adults. She walked out the door and was halfway across the porch when she heard Mrs. Colby: "And there's no reason for you to come calling for Marcella. She won't be playing with you any more." Cheryl walked on down the steps.

"Didn't you hear me?" Mrs. Colby called after her.

Cheryl waited until she reached the front walk before she turned. "Oh, yes, ma'am. I did hear you."

Mrs. Colby closed the door and went into the kitchen. "What next," she sighed, pulling her Midol down from the shelf.

Upstairs, Marcella rolled over, the pillow damp from her crying. It was so unfair, her mother, *This is the Arm - y, Mis - ter Jones,* taking the slip away from her before she could even finish explaining, *No pri - vate rooms or tel - e - phones,* how she would wash it out, clean as new. The lipstick would come out, she knew it. Cheryl said it would. And they could use it for dress-up, but no. Her mother would only say she was too old for that stuff, darn. Lucille got to do everything, just everything. It wasn't fair, Mrs. Colby making Marcella give away her Shirley Temple set last year, but this wasn't kid stuff. This was *real.*

As real as Rosemary Riker.

She'd seen Rosemary in her slip lots of times, they weren't very careful about who saw you in underwear at Cheryl's house, Cheryl and Rosemary and Lynn parading around almost in their altogether, *Oh, the girls in France*, in front of brothers, and everything. Marcella wasn't even supposed to go there any more, so she always had to ditch Lucille first.

Rosemary, dressed like a grownup, with her pompadour hairdo and her puckered slip, trimmed so pretty, with lacy neck and scalloped hem, and silky. So unfair! And she in her cotton undershirt, all flattened down. *Oh, the girls in France, Do the hootch – y kootch – y dance! And the way they shake* she could be wearing the slip this minute, except Lucille would probably find out, and tell, and then her mother really would be mad, popping mad, like she was when Lucille tattled about the coats—golly, oh, she was *furious*, and why couldn't they keep the slip, anyway? It would wash out, the "fuck you" would wash right out, and what did it mean. *Oh, the girls in France, don't wear an - y un - der - pants*, she knew it would wash out as white as snow, as white as virgins' clothes.

Cheryl told her all about virgins, and white clothes, and brides, and wearing white clothes to get married, like Ginger Rogers, and the organ sounds filling the church, and *white*. That meant only God's finger had ever touched you, but if you didn't wear white, oh-oh, that meant you weren't a *virgin*, and boy would your husband be mad! So you had to wear everything white, like a nurse, white dress, white hat, white gloves, even white underpants, that's what Cheryl said.

Everything.

That's why the slip...they hadn't even noticed the words at first, there weren't that many, "prick," what did "prick" mean, Cheryl laughing when she asked, and the handkerchiefs, white, hers, and her mother's, only they didn't know about virgins then, such a long time ago, they were only in fourth grade, or maybe fifth, still playing hopscotch and skip rope (oh, she was good at "skim the milk," she was, always good at rhythm things) and Cheryl her first real best friend ever, so she didn't have to play with Lucille all the time, Cheryl still her best friend, her only friend, waiting for each other after school, hiding from Lucille, letting the other kids go by so no one would see them. Besides, nobody would walk with them anyway, Karen and Linda and Donna not nice like her mother kept saying, but mean, always hollering things like "I see London, I see France. You've got poop in your underpants," holding their noses, and shouting *phew, phew, phew!* At first Marcella thought it was just her, and she was scared Lucille might hear them and tell, and her mother would ask, "Why can't you get along with *nice* girls," but then Marcella saw them teasing Cheryl, too, so finally she and Cheryl began to run together, and they would wait, and hide from Lucille, and let all the kids go by, maybe "prick" means poops. Cheryl says it is real dirty; kiss my poop, maybe that's what it means—ugh!

Then taking turns, Marcella first, always first because Cheryl wouldn't play unless, and scrunching the handkerchief up into a ball, after opening it all up, or else it would stay too flat when you wadded it, and then, after you make a ball, stuffing it up quick, and the other one, up the front of your sweater, laughing so hard they nearly fell off the curbstone, Cheryl, laughing and pointing, and sometimes not putting her own handkerchiefs in, even though she'd promised.

So funny.

And the slip, all wadded up when they found it, Cheryl spotting it, seeing the straps hanging out of the big tin trash can, "You first." Lick my ass. Marcella knew what that meant; ass was dirty for behind, so maybe prick was poop. Lick my ass. Kiss my prick.

And "fuck"? Fuck you? What could that be? She wondered if her mother knew. Where was her mother, anyway?

Marcella rolled off the bed, and peered down the open hot-air register, but she couldn't see a thing. Oh, well. She flopped over on her side and began rolling balls of lint from the throw rug, little balls, small enough to knit mice sweaters.

Sometimes Cheryl played it too, but mostly Marcella, first with her handkerchief on one side and Cheryl's on the other, and then they tried Kleenex, but that didn't work so well, and then they stole their mothers', just for fun. That was easy. "I need a handkerchief. Mine are all dirty," and her mother got her one.

They could do it with the slip, too, Cheryl said they could, sometime when the boys weren't home they would bring it to Cheryl's place, and take their clothes off and everything, like real, so soft and silky against the bare skin, like Rosemary's stockings had been, oh! Rosemary and Lynn, buying a pair of real silk stockings, to share, even though you aren't supposed to buy silk, with the war and everything, but they did. One pair of stockings for the both of them. Cost nearly $3, that's what Cheryl said, and the stockings were bright green, to match a dress Rosemary had, and they thought they were such big deals, wearing silk. "Strutting their stuff, that's all they think about," Cheryl scoffed, but she and Marcella tried the stockings on once, when no one was home.

How *thin* they were, how limp, and sheer, Marcella afraid she'd rip them, Cheryl saying brother she'd really get it if there was a snag, they were ever so careful, first Marcella, and then Cheryl.

After that they made the pact.

Oh, it was super secret—dibs, double dibs, triple dibs, cross your fingers twice behind your back and swear never to tell, never *ever*, stick a needle in your eye, cross your heart and hope to die before you say. *That* kind of a secret, and of course they didn't tell Lucille.

They each stole two, but not right away. They talked about it first. "You're chicken," Cheryl kept saying, and "What the matter, got ants in your pants?" and Marcella said no, but she was scared, she really was, tiptoeing into her mother's big bedroom where she was never supposed to go without permission. She got caught, once, the rubber heels on her new Easter shoes, fake rubber because of the war, those stupid heels leaving long black streaks across her mother's polished floor. Ruining the finish! What a fuss Mrs. Colby made when she saw it, making Marcella erase it all, every mark, even though Lucille had done some of them, Marcella was *sure* she had, but Lucille *never* got punished, oh, no, Daddy's little favorite, Lucille could do no wrong, so Marcella had to erase them *all*, down on her hands and knees with a pencil eraser, rubbing, rubbing, one at a time, and what if her shoes should do it again, tiptoeing over to the bureau where her father kept his, she knew which drawer, the top one, on the left-hand side, and lifting the handles ever so quietly. She thought she'd never finish, and that her mother would for sure catch her up there, but finally she stole two, two of them, hiding them under her clothes, leaving them there, not taking them out at breakfast or on the way to school because of Lucille. Lucille would ask what they were for, so the handkerchiefs stayed there, flat as cummerbunds, until recess when she showed Cheryl she was *not* chicken, stuffing them in her coat pocket until she could hide them in her desk, waiting, keeping them there, until Cheryl stole hers, too.

Should she go downstairs now? Maybe not. Her mother might still be mad. Better stay in her room until suppertime, make believe she'd been reading or something.

But fuck couldn't mean pee, that didn't make sense, pee you, and they didn't say fuck *on* you, so it wasn't pee. Maybe it meant touching, not the finger of God, of course, but the other: "Don't let the boys *touch* you," Mrs. Colby kept saying, so maybe fuck meant touch, and you'd have to wear red or blue at your wedding and everyone would laugh.

They dawdled longer than usual, that day, to make triple sure no one saw them, and then—shaking out the big men's handkerchiefs, Cheryl's father's was brown-and-white plaid, and her father's all white, monogrammed with a Bible-lettered capital C, and wadded them up into. Such *big* balls. Oh, huge as *cantaloupes!*

"You first," said Cheryl, and Marcella did, stuffing and stuffing: so big her sweater lifted way high at the waist. "Ooooooh! Hoooooooo! You can see your belly!" Cheryl squealing, covering up her mouth and pointing, squirming with laughter. *Oh, the girls in France,* but Marcella didn't care, and stuffed the other one up too, oh, hoooooo, hooooooo, how funny they looked, bobbing in the air, like Rosemary's, and so heavy!

They wouldn't stay up, not even under sweaters—of course the little hankies slip right down under blouses and dresses, but sweaters, usually fine, never fall down, but these melons! Not even sweaters could hold them, but maybe the slip could, because of its pouches, that's what Cheryl said, they'd put hankies in the pouches, and then a belt, pulled tight so they won't slide down or anything, oh!

They decided to wear their coats inside out, and strut their stuff like Lynn and Rosemary, so Marcella turned her dusty blue winter coat around, pulling one sleeve through, and then the other, so only the royal blue quilted lining showed, and Cheryl's a sort of wine red. "That means we're not virgins," Cheryl said. But it wasn't true! My, how shiny the linings were, satin, she thought, but maybe only rayon like the slip was, soft as the slip, and shining when they walked along, pretending they were "Which Twin Has the Toni" girls, wearing their coats inside out, and open, so you could see what they had under there, but keeping their hands on the coats in case, *Do the hootch – y kootch – y dance,* so they could close them up quick if anybody came by, and it was a good thing they did, because Lucille was spying on them. Trying to keep the hankies up there, but not able to, and sometimes one breast *up,* and one *down,* ooooooooh, hoooooooo, and Lucille tattling on them, only not about the hankies, just about the coats.

"Why don't you ask your mother what it means?" Fuck you! Up yours! "Ask your mother." That's what Cheryl said. "She'll tell you." Lick my ass! Hooooooooo! Hooooooooo!

Hildreth is the county seat, and largest town, in Phelps County, Kansas. In 1945 it had twelve churches, or enough to attend a new church each month. That is not, of course, as many churches as Cholula, Mexico, had in its heyday. Legend says Cholula had three hundred and sixty-five churches, or enough to attend one a day. But those were Catholic, so they don't count.

Mrs. Colby collected a handful of wooden matches from the kitchen and headed across the backyard to the alley incinerator. How like Cheryl Riker to be in on it. Disgusting. Disgusting filth. Like animals, these high school boys, nothing but trash, any of them, worse than animals, at least animals do it from instinct, but these boys, mostly farm boys anyway, nothing but filthy pigs, watching the bulls do it, of course they have to watch, that's part of their job, but still. Mounting the calves themselves, some said. The Stock boys, oh, it was too revolting to be true. She shouldn't even listen to such smut, could never get it out of her mind. Downright ruffians, all of them! A good thing Warren doesn't know. If he did, like as not he and his courthouse cronies would set out to show those boys a thing or two. Or get shown. He's getting too old for such shenanigans.

I suppose, she comforted herself, Marcella was lucky in a way. Could have been worse. Could have been what she thought it was: *blood.* Monthly blood. Or maniacal—like that oldest Stock boy, going plumb crazy, climbing up the grain elevator and gunning people down, ping, ping, ping, as if they were only pheasants scurrying along some country road. People out here capable of anything, not decent, like people back home, in the East.

She ignited the slip in four separate places, then dropped it into the rusty tin incinerator. Red flame tongues leaped up, licking the silky white, slowly melting the offensive words. There was no understanding it. Those farm boys come into church every Sunday like Christians. Means nothing. Nothing at all. When they could come out and do something like…Suppose she should have cleaned it up, put it in the box for the clothes drive, but no telling who might see it. That lipstick would never come out.

She watched the heat waves rise from the barrel and glimmer in the spring air. Green. As far as she could see. Green hedges lining alleyways, grassy yards, spirea bushes, leaved trees. But it was only a sham. Nothing grows out here, not naturally anyway, bud going to leaf and back to seed again only by virtue of the irrigation well. None of it, not well, not home, not church, not tree nor yard, any protection against brutality.

She shuddered. The slip was burning, its edges black and curling, bits of charcoal ash spinning into the air. She could never get used to it, the prairie, so strange and violent. Twisting things out of their natural shapes. Even people. Yet remaining so immutable: its brutality, always there, restrained, latent even, yet always around, somehow, held delicately in check until…like that Stock boy.

Or like tornadoes. First the calm vacuum, the total stillness, turning the air hollow, and then the cloud, the long black funnel materializing, twirling, dropping, then touching down, striking viciously, striking viciously out of *nowhere*, plucking chickens to the skin, uprooting century-old trees, spinning two-storied houses through the air; screaming people clinging to...*nothing*, desperate to squeeze their fingers around a weed, a blade of grass, *anything*. But there was...nothing. No salvation. Not anywhere.

The embers turned to ash, hot black ashes sinking into the plateau of cold gray ones. She stirred them until she could see no residue, not a thread. She stirred them once more, to make sure. Then she returned to the kitchen, stopping at the sink to lather her hands thoroughly with Palmolive soap, cream them with Jergens Lotion. It was done.

C, E, G, C, E, G, C. Up and down, up and down, Marcella's fingers rippled over the piano keys so rapidly that the scales sounded almost like a harp. If only she were really playing a harp: *I come to the gar – den a – lone, while the dew is still on the* No! No! First the arpeggios, then the John Thompson, ugh. C, E, G, C, E, G, C, E, G, up, up, way up to the top of the keyboard, then down again, pell-mell.

Her fingers ached.

This is the Arm – y, Mis – ter Jones. No pri – vate rooms or tel – e phones...that's the song her father liked. Easy to play, only one flat, and the tune not hard to follow, but she didn't play it much. It reminded her of Sad Sack, sitting on his pile of potatoes, wishing he were home. And of herself, sitting on the front stoop on summer nights, listening to her father brag about when he was a kid, those awful tales, about how he tied two cats' tails together and tossed them over the clothesline and let them fight it out. About how he and his brothers strapped Uncle Ray to the top of the windmill. "You think those Stock boys are bad," he'd laugh.

His stories made her shudder.

Mr. Colby's other favorite was "Praise the Lord and Pass the Ammunition," but Marcella never played that one. Too fast. Besides, her mother hated it. Sacrilegious, Mrs. Colby called it, because it brought the Lord right into the fighting. But Mr. Colby said nonsense, how could it be sacrilegious, the song was written by a minister, for goodness sake, and Mrs. Colby said never mind, the Devil comes in strange forms sometimes, so Marcella never played it for that reason, too. No point in angering God. She got in plenty of trouble as it was. Like that slip. And she still didn't know what fuck meant, how she wanted to know, she had to know, she hated Cheryl laughing at her. What if she asked Rosemary, but Rosemary would only call her a kid, and probably laugh, and maybe even tell Lynn and then they'd both laugh.

Marcella started her second set of scales, this one in F major. F stood for flat. One flat. B. That's what Mrs. Robinson said. F for…her fingers moved uncertainly over the keys, looking for the staring place, F for…fuck anyway, oh! There was that word again, leaping into her mind, and of course she couldn't ask Lucille who was too young to know and would only tattle, and her father would laugh, she knew he would, or get so mad, and how could she ever ask her mother? F, A, C, F, A, C, F, A, C. Or maybe she could. Maybe her mother wouldn't get upset if Marcella asked the right way. Whatever that might be. *Oh, the girls in France, Do the hootch – y kootch – y dance! And the way they shake, Is e – nough to break a cake.* Maybe she would ask anyway. Her hands thundered down, down, down.

She practiced the scale until her fingers got stiff, and then she pulled her red-and-white John Thompson book out and looked for "Dark Eyes." There. It was her lesson for last week, and she had to do it over. Stupid song.

"Not animated enough," Mrs. Robinson said. "It's a gypsy dance. You're supposed to play it with fiery abandon. You must practice it slowly, each hand by itself for three or four days, and then put them together. Didn't you practice?"

Of course she'd practiced, she didn't mind that, she liked playing the piano, not like Lucille. Lucille hated it. She couldn't even play, only "Chopsticks," and that silly dog song: *Once I had a lit – tle dog. And Bing – o was his name, O. B – I – NGO, B – I – NGO, B – I – NGO, And Bing – o was his name, O.* Mrs. Colby even let Lucille stop taking lessons, but practice, practice, practice, that's all she ever said to Marcella.

"Dark Eyes" was hard. It had three flats and preparatory exercises for each hand, and maybe she'd have played it better last week if she hadn't found this really beautiful song in the Eternal Life section of the hymnal: *How hap – py ev – ery child of grace, Who knows his sins for – given!* Key of C, no sharps or flats. *"This earth," he cries, "is not my place, I seek my place in heaven."* So beautiful, playing it made her want to weep, and her mother hadn't even noticed that it wasn't "Dark Eyes." So maybe Marcella practiced the hymn a little more than she had her lesson.

Anyway, Cheryl thought it was dopey, playing church songs.

Oh, but "How Happy" made the piano sound like an organ, like a real church organ, especially if you held the pedal down a lot, and not "sparingly" like Mrs. Robinson kept saying.

Cheryl thought Marcella should play sheet music songs like "When You Wish Upon a Star," that was Cheryl's favorite, or "Woodie Woodpecker's Song." But Marcella couldn't. Her mother wouldn't let her. Mrs. Colby said those Hit Parade songs were nothing but trash, and she wouldn't let her own daughters listen to the Top 10 tunes of the Week, so Marcella always had to ask Cheryl what the Number One song was. That made her so mad. Her mother listened to pop music, Marcella knew she did. "Red Sails in the Sunset," that was Mrs. Colby's favorite. She'd even bought a record of it, a black record, too, not the unbreakable red kind.

First one hand, then the other, Marcella struggled with "Dark Eyes." Then she put them together, and when she (finally!) was done, she began practicing her very favorite in the whole world song, about meeting Jesus in the Garden, and walking and talking with Him, oh, even though it had four flats, still she knew the tune. That made it easier. She could hear the words as she played, imagining Jesus' Garden to be a little like "The Secret Garden," with morning mist over everything as she tiptoed in. *I come to the gar – den a – lone,* she was listening to the words when it popped in, just like that, *I come to the gar – den a – lone FUCK!,* right into the song like fuck was part of it. That word! It shattered the picture in her mind. She decided to ignore it, playing on, listening: *While the dew is still on the ros – es.* But the word didn't stop. *And the voice I hear FUCK!* She couldn't believe her ears, bad words becoming part of the song like those silly *oh, say can you see, any bed – bugs on me* words creep into "The Star-Spangled Banner," *if you do, pick a few, and put them on you,* but bedbugs were funny, not like this, so she tried again. She tried hard: *And the voice I hear, KISS MY, Fall – ing on my ear, KISS MY PRICK! The Son of God...*but it was no good, trying to continue. What if God Himself should hear her, those awful words right in the middle of a church song.

She stopped playing.

The slip, that slip, those words, why wouldn't they leave her a - lone? Spoiling everything! She had to find out that they meant, somehow. But how?

Maybe if she asked Reverend Chettenforth. Oh, no, if they were dirty, he probably wouldn't even know what they meant.

Maybe God. Maybe God would help her, tell her who to ask, if she prayed to Him. She didn't think so. God never paid too much attention to her, or to her prayers, not that she said prayers all that often anyway, just when she remembered to, and besides, if fuck is such a bad word you probably can't say it in a prayer. She guessed she'd have to ask her mother after all.

So Marcella hung around Mrs. Colby, waiting for the right moment to ask. She helped her mother polish the silverware— not real silver, of course, only silverplate, but Roger Bros., almost as good. She listened to her mother talk about what she would buy after the war: a new Crosley Frigidaire, the kind with all the shelves in the door so you don't have to stand on your head every time you want a jar of mustard. And a set of good china from the Ben Franklin Five-and-Dime, a set with gold trim and a covered vegetable bowl.

Marcella didn't hear any good openings, but at least Lucille wasn't around to spoil things, so she just listened, stacking the knives and forks and spoons into their hollow places in the blue velvet-lined case, putting the case away in the narrow buffet drawer, alongside the ration books and the war bonds.

Then she helped start supper—meatloaf and baked potatoes. Marcella got some dried bread crusts from the brown paper sack under the sink, and rolled the crusts into crumbs with the heavy wooden rolling pin. She watched Mrs. Colby begin to mix the crumbs with the hamburger—seven ration points a pound this week, her mother said, as bad as pork chops—and milk, with a dash of salt and pepper.

Marcella still couldn't think of a way to introduce the subject of fuck, so she rubbed some potatoes with oleo, instead, listening to her mother talk about what it was like before you could color oleo yellow with those little red-orange pellets, wrapped in cellophane. No one would eat it when it first came out, her mother said, because it looked like lard. Just like nobody would put karo syrup, clear as mineral oil, on their pancakes until Mrs. Colby added colored maple flavoring.

"It's all in the mind," Mrs. Colby said, patting the meat into a loaf. "Karo is every bit as sweet as maple syrup, and oleo tastes exactly like butter." She popped the meatloaf into the oven, and twirled the minute minder. It still didn't seem like the right time to say anything, so Marcella finished rubbing the potatoes, carefully puncturing their skins with a fork before she put them in the oven.

Then they did the dishes. There were a lot, from lunch and from starting supper. It was Lucille's turn to dry, but Marcella didn't mention it. She kept on trying to figure out how to find out what fuck meant without coming right out and asking, but she couldn't think. She'd have to find out soon, or the dishes would be done, and Mrs. Colby would go read a book, or knit, and she hated to be interrupted then. Marcella was almost ready to give up when it came to her. How to bring the subject up. She'd have to mention Cheryl, that was risky, but…she finished drying the glass, and inverted it on the green-and-white checkered towel, before she ventured:

"You know what Cheryl says? Cheryl says 'gosh' and 'golly' aren't even swears." Mrs. Colby's back stiffened slightly. Marcella hurried on:

"And Cheryl isn't the only one. Some kids say that 'gosh' and 'darn' are only fooling-around words. They don't mean anything." This would set her mother off, she knew it would, and then she could ask…Sure enough!

"Well, let me tell you, Marcella, saying those words is just the same as taking the Lord's name in vain. It's every bit as bad as stronger profanity, and I won't have it." Mrs. Colby stopped washing dishes long enough to look at her daughter. "How many times must I tell you, 'gosh' is nothing but the colloquial form for 'God,' and so is 'golly,' just as 'darn' is slang for 'damn.' It's a thin veneer. And if the good Lord doesn't make a distinction between 'darn' and 'damn,' neither should you." She returned to her suds.

Marcella was at a loss. If her mother got that upset about golly, whatever would she say to fuck? But how could such a touchy subject be brought up another time? And when? Oh, Marcella had to find out! So she asked:

"Is fuck a swear?"

Mrs. Colby clapped a plate in the drainer before she answered, "Worse than any swear word you could ever swear. Worse then blasphemy. I don't want to ever hear you say that word again. Especially around Lucille. I don't want Lucille coming in here asking about it, either, do you hear?"

Marcella nodded. Cheryl was right, then. It was really bad. Even worse than killing God. Oh, but she *had* to know...

"What does it *mean*, anyway?"

Her mother was silent for so long Marcella was afraid she might not answer. When she did, she spoke slowly:

"It means nothing, nothing at all. It's just a dirty word, a dirty sex word that some farm boys made up. There is no need to use it, and I don't want to hear it ever again spoken in this house. Is that clear?"

Marcella nodded.

They worked in silence for a time. Mrs. Colby's chore ball was scrubbing the bottom of the frying pan when Marcella ventured again.

"But why is it worse than a curse?"

Mrs. Colby plunged the frying pan in and out of the soapy water, and rinsed it, and handed it to Marcella before she answered: "Well, cursing is extremely bad in itself. Taking the name of the Lord in vain is the first thing forbidden in the Ten Commandments, even before murder. But words like the one you ask about are much worse than ordinary profanity because, they aren't simply curses. They are filthy ones."

She inverted the dishpan, not even waiting for the water to be sucked down the drain before she began scouring, scouring the sink.

2

Marcella was up in her room, playing, when she heard Mr. Colby's Packard pull into the driveway. "Suppertime," she thought, putting her things away, and heading down the hall. But something was wrong. She heard the crying even before she reached the top of the stairs. She walked slowly down, caution stiffening her limbs. It was her mother. Marcella could see her, crouching in the overstuffed rocker, her shoulders shaking, her hands covering her face. Marcella had never seen her mother cry before.

"What's the matter?" she asked.

"The President died," Mr. Colby said.

They didn't eat a regular supper that night, only cereal, which their father fixed for them because Mrs. Colby went to bed early. The world could never be the same without President Roosevelt and his Fireside Chats, Mr. Colby explained over the Cheerios.

The funeral was on Saturday. Nobody from Hildreth went, because Washington was so far away, but everybody listened to it on the radio. Even the stores closed down.

Then it was May, and Lucille got five May baskets and Marcella got none, but she didn't care. A bunch of silly kid stuff, anyway, and then, hooray, the war was *over*, or almost.

It was V-E Day, and she and Lucille marched all around the block singing, and waving flags, and taking turns ringing a cowbell.

3

You could see them right through the school's double-glass door, but all shimmery, like looking through a mirror, sliced in half by the aluminum bar—two men, dressed in business suits, strangers. Standing on the sidewalk right next to the flagpole.

"Who are those guys anyway?" Cheryl, beside her, walking fast.

"I don't know." Remembering to put her heels down hard, so she wouldn't accidentally run, and have to stay after.

A flood of sixth graders pressed against the metal silvery rod, streamed through the door, and started, some right across the stiff brown grass, even though—

"Step on the grass," cried Cheryl, shoving her, "see your—"

"Underpants," hissed Marcella, shoving back.

But if not on the grass, then right by the men, handing out…

"If it's candy, we mustn't take any," said Marcella. Cheryl shifted so Marcella had to walk close to them. But it wasn't candy. It was paper, flimsy blue paper, with writing. Offering. Smiling. Some children reaching hands. Taking.

Cheryl poked Marcella. "You," she hissed.

"No, you," Marcella whispered back, giggling. But Marcella was always the one to go first, to tell fibs, to cover up for them—they weren't supposed to play together any more, but they did.

Marcella reached out her hand. A man, the tall one, his suit black with shiny stripes on the sleeve, handed her...and blond hairs on the back of his hand, curling over—freckles!

"There, my little chickadees," he said, smiling. The girls ran away, hearing his "Laughter is God's medicine" in the air behind them.

"Come on, let me have it," Cheryl said, but Marcella wouldn't. Let Cheryl look over *her* shoulder for once.

"CHRIST IS RISEN," the paper said. There He stood, in His robe, hands outstretched. The Risen Jesus. You could tell by the black ink holes in His hands. Where they'd pounded the nails. In the church, a picture showed it, the nails enormous, like railroad spikes, and pointed. They had to be. Hard to drive a nail through a hand, oh, harder than fishhooks through minnows, harder even than the part *after* you poke the hook through its mouth, when you twist the hook around and poke the spiky part through its body, her father showed her how. Making holes. The nail holes, black, in His hands, black as the vomit blood that came out with her tonsils, black as sin.

"Some church thing," Marcella said, excited. There wasn't usually anything to do after school except play. "The Evangelicals. Hey, Thursday, three o'clock. That's today! Let's go."

"Naw, I can't," said Cheryl. "It isn't Catholic."

"That doesn't matter. It isn't Methodist, either. Besides, Catholics are Christian, aren't they?" Marcella said it, though how could it be true, when they worship idols, like the heathens do. "Nobody would care, I know they wouldn't."

"Naw."

"Oh, come on."

"Naw."

"We don't have to tell. Nobody would even know."

"I can't."

"Please, Cheryl. Pretty please? Just this once." Marcella paused. What would make Cheryl do it? "I think it might be a revival. Have you ever been to one?"

"Nope."

"They're loads of fun. Singing. And everybody gets saved."

"What's that? Getting saved."

"Oh, you know," Marcella replied loftily. "Finding Jesus. And... and..." what could she hold out? Their churches were as off-limits to each other as the Holy Rollers were to both. The Holy Rollers. Maybe that would...

She lowered her voice.

"Sometimes they speak in tongues, you know."

"Really?"

Oh, that would do it!

"Honest and true! Cross my heart and hope to die. They shake all around, and roll, and sometimes they foam at the mouth. Old Mrs. Chandler, she saw them once. She told me."

So Cheryl waited down the block where Mrs. Colby wouldn't see her, while Marcella asked could she, and convinced her mother that Lucille was too young to go.

Marcella and Cheryl hopscotched up the cement stairs of the Evangelical Church—almost as many steps as the Phelps County Courthouse. They pushed the immense wooden doors aside.

The church was really dark after the harsh prairie sun, almost spooky. Cheryl giggled when the door creaked, until Marcella had to say "Shhhhhhhh." They tiptoed down the main aisle, almost to the front pew, but not quite, in case people in the front row had to do something.

The place was stacked with kids, maybe thirty of them. Everybody was there. But then it never took much to draw a crowd in Hildreth, there was so little to do. Marcella spotted a few Methodists, like herself.

"Hey, where are the grownups?" she whispered, but Cheryl was busy fanning herself with a paper fan from the hymn-book rack. A picture of Our Saviour was on one side and an ad for Heink's funeral parlor on the other.

"Put it back, dopey," Marcella hissed. "You aren't supposed to touch that stuff."

The service started off just like Sunday morning. A lady, dressed in a long white robe, sat at the piano and played "Holy, Holy, Holy." Marcella knew the song—page one in the Methodist's hymnal. Four sharps, key of E, E for...*God in Three Per - sons, bless - ed Trin - i - ty...*

"Just like church," she was about to tell Cheryl, when the men came out. "Hey," she whispered instead. "Look at them! They've got *robes* on!" Long white robes, both like the lady's, nearly hiding their pants' legs. Those same two men, but looking like choir people now.

After the opening prayer—the big blond man prayed it, in a voice as soft as whipped cream—everything was quiet. Then the lady stepped to the front of the platform and began reading from a Holy Bible lifted high in her hands, but not like Reverend Chettenforth read on Sunday mornings. Her reading was more like singing, high and clear, her voice like running water. She barely looked at the words:

"And, behold, there was a great earthquake: for the angel of the Lord descended from heaven, and came and rolled back the stone from the door..." like ghosts, it must have been, in the Garden, that morning. Marcella shivered. She became so intent, listening, that she forgot Cheryl, forgot the church, the hard pew, seeing only the lady's face, her face, so lovely, she might have been an angel of the Lord herself, and hearing only her voice, cresting, deepening, how could one woman have so many voices? She veritably flung out the final words: "Fear not ye: for I know that ye seek Jesus which was crucified. He is not here: for He is risen, as He said..." Which was crucified, and dead, and buried. Marcella knew all about it, how the curtain in the temple ripped right down the middle when He died, how rocks split and everybody *knew*, only it was too late. How the women rubbed His poor body with spices, wrapping it round and round, a baby in swaddling clothes, but over His head, too, and stuck Him in a big cave, and posted guards so the disciples couldn't steal Him and *say* He Is Risen, the stone sealed so tight that *nobody* could open it, not even twelve men, and that's how we know...

Marcella began wishing Cheryl hadn't come. What if God saw Cheryl sitting beside her, and remembered "fuck" and the other bad stuff? She edged away.

But they were singing, the three of them, the men's voices deep and low, the woman's all soft and high like the Heavenly Host, *There is a foun – tain filled with blood*...from His hands, of course. And from His poor body where a Roman soldier stuck his spear oh! *And sin – ners, plunged be – neath that flood, Lose all their guilt – y stains*...and the soldiers, teasing Jesus, giving Him only vinegar to drink. And not breaking His legs. Because if they *had*, how could Christ walk among us again, the Christ Risen, but Jesus died pretty fast, that was part of God's plan, so the soldier took out his spear and gashed Jesus' side, *Thy flow – ing wounds sup – ply*, you can still see the scar in a picture in the church basement, but the robbers weren't so lucky. The soldiers, carrying huge sticks with iron balls on one end. Smashing the robbers' legs. Blood. Pieces of bone sticking through flesh—ugh! She tried not to think about it, *Dear dy – ing Lamb, Thy pre –*

cious blood…all running red, oh, there must have been a ton of it, He was so much bigger than Mrs. Schneider's chickens, when she chopped their heads off, like the drinking fountain at school when you put your thumb over half of it and step way back, so you won't get drenched, that's how the blood of Mrs. Schneider's chickens flowed, and His body, jerking. How that must have hurt when they lifted the cross, His body dangling by the nails, and ker – *thunk*, down into the hole that had been dug for it, oh! How hurt! More than the robbers, their hands tied with rope, but oh! The robbers! their poor broken legs, ow! *Lies si – lent in the grave.*

They were finished.

Then the blond man stepped forward and introduced himself, Brother Morgan was his name. He began to talk. Such strange talk, not teacher talk, always explaining, or church talk, preaching, preaching, and not like regular grown-up talk at all. Hushed, and low, like when you play the piano with the soft pedal dampening the keys, so low Marcella had to lean forward to hear, about Jesus, in the Temple, His folks searching high and low for Him. But He was nowhere to be found.

"Like some kids I know when there are dishes to be done," and Cheryl, giggling, but so were some other kids so that was okay, and about how Jesus was only twelve years old when that happened.

"Yes, sir, my little ones, only twelve, but Jesus gave up His childish ways and grew up into the Son of God He really was, like we are all sons of God, sons and daughters of the Lord God Almighty, just waiting for Him to come along and call."

Suddenly he was shouting:

"How many twelve-year-olds here? How many? Let me see those hands."

So many hands, going up, even Ginny Preston's, and she was only eleven, and some kids in the seventh and eighth grades put their hands up, too, and he was calling:

"How many thirteen? And older? Let me see those hands! How many people here are old enough to stand up for God? Let's see! Let's see you stand up for God."

And everybody standing, waving their hands in the air, even Cheryl, and some boys stood on pews, but others dragged them down, and suddenly everyone was singing *Stand up, stand up for Je - sus, Ye sol - diers of the cross,* even if they didn't remember all the words, everybody chiming in on the *stand up* part, and on the *lift high His roy - al ban - ner* part, raising their hands way up in the air like Brother Morgan's.

Everybody felt better after that.

Then the lady got up and said, "Hello. My name is May, and I'm Brother Morgan's wife." She told them about how she used to wear lipstick, and smoke, and drink, and let boys kiss her and everything. But how God was her Father, all right. He pulled her right into a church service, "just like God pulled you in here today, don't think that was an accident." She told them how Brother Morgan was in that church, and how he'd shown her the way to God's Grace, just like he would show everyone here today, it was so easy. And she didn't smoke, or drink, or do any of those other things any more. Oh, if only Lucille were here, if only she could listen to this, maybe she'd stop fighting, and lying, and carrying tales...

Then the dark man jumped up, all hunched over and talking in a sing-song voice, saying things like, "Oh, God, then I was chained, but now I am free, oh, yes, dear Jesus, thank you so much, then I was blind, but now I see," telling how he used to be a cripple, not really a cripple hunched over like he is, pretending to be, but that he might as well have been because there was so much hate in his soul, all hate and not a drop of loving in it, oh, no, not until Jesus came and loved his hate away, took it all away, and washed him, washed him in His precious blood until he was so clean, clean as snow, as fresh as the driven snow…and he was standing tall again.

Then Brother Morgan took his turn, talking about Peter denying he knew the Lord, and then about Thomas, oh, Thomas, all the time doubting, as bad as Simon Peter ever was. He did not believe. "Until I put my finger into the print of the nails," Thomas said, "until I thrust my hand into the hole in His side, I am not going to believe." Oh, Thomas, how could you *not* believe, three days under the rock and then risen, so God could pardon all our sins, all the sins of the world.

"WHAT ARE WE WAITING FOR?" Brother Morgan really began to shout. "WHAT IS IT THAT WE WANT? ARE WE WAITING, LIKE THOMAS, TO PLACE OUR FINGERS IN THE HOLE IN HIS PRECIOUS HAND? MUST WE HAVE THAT KIND OF PROOF? ARE WE WAITING UNTIL JESUS HIMSELF COMES BEFORE US, OFFERING US HIS WOUNDED SIDE TO RECEIVE OUR DOUBTING HANDS?"

The silence, after he stopped, was so enormous it rang in Marcella's ears. She wanted to glance at Cheryl, but she was too scared to move. Then all three of them, Brother Morgan and his wife and the dark man, were talking, all at once, sort of, not so much talking as chanting, come, come now, oh come and taste the Lord's sweet mercy, come kneel at His feet, come let Him lay His hands on you, and heal you.

The three of them stood straight and tall, their hands stretched out like the Christ risen on the paper. They swayed back and forth, back and forth, saying, oh, sweet Jesus, I am yours, all yours, chanting so soft and low. Then Brother Morgan's voice rose up above the rest:

"Oh, come now, yes come now, you are old enough, come, come, leave your mother and your father and cleave to Him who truly loves you, yes, my little ones, tell the Lord how sorry you feel about the things you've done, yes, yes, about how bad you've been, a-men, Lord, haven't we all, a-men, but that doesn't matter any more, O Lord, for He is calling, yes, God is calling, yes, you, and He is saying, come, come, walk right down that aisle, walk right down front, He is saying, and let Brother Morgan lay his hands on you, listen to Him, you stood up for me, He is saying, now walk for me, right down this aisle, come, come, come..."

Calling, then, for someone brave enough to be the first, calling for someone brave enough to walk right down that aisle and show God how much he loves Him, and Marcella, so scared, wondering if God would call her first. Wondering if God would call her at all. Maybe He would call Cheryl, instead, looking all around, but with her head still bowed so God would pass her by, she didn't want to be first, and wanting to walk right down that aisle, but afraid to, not knowing if it was okay, remembering all those swears, and all those dirty jokes she and Cheryl swapped, and promising never ever again, dibs double-dibs, I really mean it this time, and Brother Morgan still chanting, yes, oh yes, brother, come forward, now, and Mrs. Morgan and the dark man still holding out their hands, come, come, and everyone sort of swaying and nodding when big Lucas Stock, nearly sixteen, came stumbling down the aisle, his face so red.

Brother Morgan, putting his hands on Lucas's shoulders, and kind of showing him how he should kneel down in front of everybody, and the dark man, still chanting, "Come, come to the Lord," like it was the easiest thing in the world, and Mrs. Morgan, going to the piano, and playing, and other kids, walking down the aisle, some quietly, some sort of noisy, banging against pews as they clambered out, she'd have to go so soon, if she was going to go, and Marcella, trying to bow her head and pray, but she couldn't.

How the music, oh, how the chanting made her head tingle, and her heart, how pounding! What was it? it seemed mostly inside her, she could feel it, inside, mostly in her knees, yes, and flowing over her calves, was it the music? Or could it be? Oh! She began trembling, all over, her arms, and her legs, trembling, just like she'd shake if the Lord should appear to her in all His Glory yes! so sharply it almost hurt, but more like caressing, a funny shaky sort of feeling, or was it her skin crawling from the music, the way it was ebbing, and now, rising, pushing its way through her oh! whole body! Even unto her fingertips, curved tight around the pew, could it be God? making them uncurl? calling? and her knees, unbending oh! it must be! and her gaze, lifting, to Brother Morgan, in his white robe, calling, yes, calling, his eyes seeking out all those who, like herself, and calling, yes, His eyes, looking only at hers, and the music, cresting, and the trembling, yes! yes! it *had* to be! God, calling, her, even *her*! and her face, her whole face flushing, afraid to turn and look at Cheryl for her face was all over on fire, and Cheryl would surely see.

Then she knew it was her turn, that she was next to go down the aisle, and she started, stumbling over Cheryl on the way. Cheryl grabbed her dress and hissed, "Sit *down*, Marcella," but there was no stopping her, oh, no, for God had called her, her personally, and she was not about to turn Him down.

Afterward, the saved had to stay. They all filed into the dusty back room where Mrs. Morgan and the dark man had hung up their robes. The three of them seemed different, somehow. The dark man was saying, "I've got to run. Have to get those flyers over to the power plant before four thirty or we're finished." Mrs.

Morgan was shuffling through her purse for the car keys, and trying to quiet two small boys. Brother Morgan stood watching her, and teasing: 'You know how God punished Adam? He made him keep Eve."

"Oh, Jim," said Mrs. Morgan, sort of cross.

Then everybody signed a piece of paper saying they'd been saved, and what their regular church was, and everybody got a copy of the New Testament, it didn't matter whether you already had one or not, it was a memo of the day you'd been saved. "A little souvenir from the Lord," Brother Morgan joked, and he showed them the space to sign their names, right under where he'd put his.

The testament was beautiful: a little one, small enough to hold in one hand, and bound with gold, each page edged, too. But the really lovely thing was the cover: it was white, all white, as white as the altar, and the robes, and the candles, but it was leather. Pure leather, all knobby to the touch, with nothing else on the cover except the words "New Testament" printed in gold.

Cheryl was waiting beside the big cement steps.

"Did they make you wash in blood?" she asked. "No," Marcella said, and showed her the Testament, but she wouldn't let Cheryl touch it. They started toward home, skirting the Colby block so Mrs. Colby wouldn't see them together.

"How come you wouldn't go down front?" Marcella asked. She wondered if she should play with Cheryl any more. It had seemed all right before, dodging Lucille, hiding from her mother, fibbing. But now –

"I don't know," Cheryl said, shaking her head funny, like she was trying to knock a fly off of her cheek or something. "I wasn't even supposed to be in there, you know. Hey, listen, remember that story I was going to tell you? After school, but those guys were out front, and we didn't have time?"

"Yah," Marcella said, beginning to feel uncomfortable. Cheryl was always wanting to tell dirty stories, and Marcella was usually ready to top them, but here, with the white Bible in her hand—

"Well, it's about this little egg," Cheryl said, and already she was giggling, tucking her face down toward her collar. "This little egg…"

Marcella halted.

"Stop it," she shouted. "You just stop it, Cheryl Riker. How can you say such a dirty filthy…"

Cheryl stood staring, her face full of her surprise.

"Well, you know, I just got *saved*. So things are different now."

4

Marcella lay flat on her back in the white enamel tub. The bubble-bath suds had almost vaporized, leaving wispy traces of film and scattered conglomerations of bubbles, clinging together like fish eggs…. She blew a still concealed group, scattering it across her belly. How flat her breasts were! As though still a kid, like Lucille, as though she could run around outdoors without a T-shirt, as though she could, could even pass for a boy, except…of course, boys had

Well, God just made them different, that's all. Down there. Under their B.V.D.'s…what did they have, actually? she didn't know, exactly, except that dogs' were all furry. She'd seen a baby's, once. His was tiny, a little fire hydrant, squirting water straight up to the ceiling, his mother not even mad, but giggling, grabbing a towel, "Oh, they always do it when you take the diaper off!"

Except girls. Girls don't do things like that. Not even Cheryl. She didn't play much with Cheryl any more.

Her nipples, flat pale circles again her skin, like they used to be, and she could pretend, lying flat in the tub like this, she could pretend that none of it had happened, none at all: not the breasts, not the hair, in her armpits, or the hair, down there, already sprouting. It was harder to pretend with the hair, so much of it, all over, and tickly. Had to wear deodorant sometimes. Mum. Sharing her mother's white glass jar, not letting anyone watch, especially not Lucille, dipping a finger in. Cool, white stuff, sticking to her finger after she'd rubbed it on, matting her underarm hair like wet cat fur, oh, but she could still pretend that the arm hair was gone, she could make it disappear, squeezing her arms tight together and poking the straggling hair back in the crack. She hated her hair. It made her feel funny, and she had to wipe the extra Mum on her *leg*, a little egg, ran up her... "Not on *cloth*, it can stain cloth," her mother said, catching Marcella wiping her finger on her panties. But the breasts, that part wasn't so bad, that part was nice.

How delicious, bathing in the middle of the afternoon. That was the nice thing about summer, not having to hurry up in the bathroom, so much different from school mornings when you have to finish, so Lucille can brush her teeth. Not seeing Cheryl was easier, now that school was done. She turned over, slosh, slowly, arching her back, letting her shoulders drop, watching the water run in rivulets down her sides.

Her breasts were biggest this way. They seemed like honest-to-goodness grown-up breasts, hanging way down, almost like Rosemary's, Rosemary's so enormous, she'd seen them once, *enormous*, big as muskmelons, well nearly. So much bigger than Marcella's little buds. Where do breasts go, anyway, when you lie down flat in the tub? Do Rosemary's ooze off her chest like big gobs of melting ice cream? Do they go flat? But not her nipples, oh no! The nipples of Rosemary as big around as pennies, as nickels, you bet, not like these little pencil stub things of Marcella's, but huge...

Marcella swung her breasts, sleigh bells ringing in the bath water, sploosh, splosh. Breasts are so easy to understand, everybody has them. Some of the sixth grade girls, you can see nipples sticking through their blouses, Cheryl giggled at them—

she and Cheryl were still best friends at recess, and in the water line—and cats, even cats have them, tiny pink dots in rows on their furry stomachs, and chickens, no, not chickens, baby chicks just scratch in the dust for bugs, right from the beginning, but cows! Cows are something else! Those udders, they are breasts, cow breasts, one weird breast all hooked together, in a gigantic— bouquet. Huge. So heavy with milk, heavy as the bottles left on the porch every morning, and the cows, bumpety, bum, bump, swaying along, not cute like Elsie at all, cows, wobbling when they try to move, their tail bones sticking up through their fur like skulls. It must hurt when they walk, that continual... shuddering, after they come to a halt. And the nipples, oh, cow nipples are bigger than thumbs, you can put your whole hand around a cow's nipple, if you want to, who would want to? Their skin scratchy as a snake's, but the calves don't mind.

She slid forward, leaning her warm cheek against the tub's cool white side. Cool as ice. Her mother only said she wasn't supposed to play with Cheryl, but they could still walk. Was it all right to walk home together after school?

The thing that is hard to figure is the thing they *do*. How do they do it? The thing that fuck meant, oh, she knew, she figured it out, finally. It means the thing that you do to make babies. But how do they do it? With a seed, that's what Cheryl said, the man has a seed, but Marcella still didn't understand it. The man must get the seed and hold it in his hand, or maybe with tweezers, until he has a chance to do it. He must have to touch you, somehow, maybe holding you while he makes you swallow it, maybe it tastes awful, even fuzzy, or maybe it goes in some other way, like dogs, no! Cheryl says a dog sticks its furry thing right inside the mother! Oh yes they do, she said, when Marcella protested, and if you scare them when they're doing it, they stick together, and you've got to take them to the vet to get them unstuck, oh, but people don't do it like *that*. How could they? People must do it like robins, sitting side-by-side on branches, and rubbing their feathers together. How *awful* if people did it like dogs, and who would unstick them if they got stuck? The doctor? No, it must be the other way, swallowing the seed, and maybe rubbing, too. Yes, when they wanted Marcella, then her father must have gotten the seed, and given it to her mother, that sounded right, and then again, when they wanted Lucille.

The enamel of the tub began to feel hard. Maybe she would hurry up and wash, then go outdoors and find Lucille. Or play the piano. Or...she didn't feel like reading. Marcella sat up, turned the steaming water on, feeling it strike hot and low between her feet, watching the hundreds of bubbles shimmer up, waiting until her feet turned bright red and she couldn't stand it one second longer before she turned the water off, then scooping it, oar-like, back along the two boat sides of her body. Or...

Soaping. Woodbury soap.

"Start at the top," her mother always said, "so you don't have to rinse your face with dirty feet water."

Marcella couldn't see what difference it made, feet and legs and even your behind, all right in the water along with the rest. She started at the top just the same, soaping with her hands, eyes squinched shut, wringing the washcloth almost dry before wiping suds off her face. Opening one eye, experimentally, and then the other. No sting. Death where is thy. Then...lathering.

Down the arms, lathering the soap into white lather gloves on her hands, working more and more slowly, so much soap, and then layering it, on one breast, on the other, oh! Lucille would be so jealous! Until she had the...whooooooooooo! Like a brassiere! Like the big white brassiere Rosemary wears! Sitting up very straight, pushing her breasts way out like the ninth-grade girls do, watching how the soap bubbles were poppeting,

poppeting, slowly vanishing, soap drying down like mud in the hot sun...what?

Quick! Someone!

Rinse it off.

But no one. It had only been her imagination after all, no footsteps sounding on the stairs. *"This earth,"* he cries...

Her breasts were Rinso Bright clean, glistening with water, cool, the bath water already cooling. Scrubbing her back, her legs, her feet, in between her toes, then unplugging, white rubber plug with metal bead chain, squatting, letting the water drip off, watching the water swirl down the drain, squatting, putting her hands, one hand under each breast, hefting them. Leaning over, way over, until they grew heavy in her hands. Lift. Drop. Lift, and then, switching, up/down, down/up, up/down, like milking a cow...the water already draining with its long belching sound... always forgetting to scrub the water line until too late.

She detoured into her parents' bedroom, tiptoeing across the gleaming floor, oh, dear God in Heaven, watch over your little lamb, tiptoeing so no one downstairs would hear, the floor, not rug-covered, but bare, polished, shining like enamel. Off-limits. The room, stretching out before her, nearly as large as the living room below it, but seeming more enormous because she visited it so seldom, always getting caught if she did. Her mother, winging in like a homing pigeon to see that no one scuffed the floor, her floor, this precious hardwood floor, her prize, let no one violate it. But could it really be a sin to come in here without asking? Such a little thing. Besides, Marcella wanted to...see! Oh, naked, like Eve in the garden of plenty before the...and she read such strange things in the book of Leviticus: "Thou shalt not approach unto a woman to uncover her nakedness…It is abomination." Unclean. Unclean. But how could it be wrong? After all, God made our bodies, our bodies are the handiwork of the Lord God Almighty…and the only full-length mirror was in the master bedroom.

So she decided. She decided she would, yes, look at herself, naked, in the mirror, indeed she would…of course she hadn't really *known* she would when she tiptoed into the room, but now deciding, yes, she never *had* looked, not once, but now she would, even if it was a little sinful, like the sin of pride, maybe, and acting, as quickly now as she once moved slowly in this room, swiping handkerchiefs—poof!

Down went the robe. She stood, stark naked, from head to toe. Studiously she looked…only at her toes, standing in front of, the mirror, so she could see—herself. Naked, before the mirror, yes, naked, full-length in the looking glass, gazing only at her toes, her ankles, then her legs, bare legs. Able to see fuzzy down on them, yes, and slowly, without fully admitting what she was doing, slowly raising her eyes, as though her image were some foreign object she viewed from a great distance, lifting, her eyes, all the way to

It was brown, the hair, down there, and darker than she'd realized. She could see it, all right, it was sure enough there, not likely to disappear, no matter how hard she pretended, so much darker than the baby down on her legs…and then bravely sliding her eyes up, oh, so carefully avoiding her own gaze, up, quickly, but not high enough to see herself, looking at

Oh! *won – der – ful things in the Bib – le I see!* They were so pretty! Not like Rosemary's, not at all. Quite different. Unmistakably cone-shaped, rounded at the base and then… like the Maidenform bra ads! In the movie mags! At Cheryl's house! She never went there any more. And her nipples, how they amused her, all pink and tiny and standing up so high now, what made them do that? Oh! Once she began looking, there was no sense stopping, so she looked, over and over again, up and down her body, discovering...she was so *beautiful*! She had not expected that, no, but it was true. This new body: long and lean and almost...curvy, not shaped like an hourglass, she noticed that, maybe that would come later, still, already nipping in at the waist, she never even knew she had a waist, the way her mother packed her in clothes, in plaid skirts with suspenders, in puff-sleeved dresses with shirring on the bodices and full skirts. *This is the dear – est, That Je – sus loves me. I am so glad...*

She stood, sucking her stomach in until it became as hollow as a dancer's, pivoting, still not confronting her eyes, but looking, looking, feeling the corners of her mouth curl, imperceptibly, feeling the smile of pride creep over her, oh, the sin of pride! But why shouldn't she be proud? Hadn't God Himself given her this beautiful body? Wasn't it a gift from Him? Oh, how glad she was that she had come unto Him, with Him beside her, it didn't matter if the kids snubbed her, and her family teased, who needed them, and she looked, as humbly as possible, at her buttocks. As surprising as her breasts! Where had her big bottom gone? Oh, so big, even her father teased her about it, "that's quite a matronly spread you've got." What did that mean? She asked Mrs. Colby, but her mother laughed and said, as much to Mr. Colby as to Marcella, "Never mind! Those are just good childbearing hips, that's all." Hips! She knew what that meant, all right, so her bottom was big, too big, she had almost cried with shame, of the bigness, and that her father had noticed it, under her clothes and everything, but now: no childbearing spread here, these new hips were nut-shaped, small, dropping with as much suggestion of convex as her stomach had of concave when she sucked it in. What a miracle! What a miracle, breasts, and bodies, and

She ventured a look at her face.

Her face was nice enough, she supposed, but oh why oh why couldn't she be really gorgeous, like the Palmolive girls, with their long hair and flushed cheeks, instead of this silly bob. Oh, well, maybe when she got old enough to wear lipstick. *I am so glad*...or maybe lipstick is sinful, she couldn't remember, and she began moving back and forth, back and forth, restrictedly at first, and then more freely, *That Je – sus loves me*, looking again mostly from the neck down, *Je – sus loves me*, watching her body move, *Je – sus loves me*, watching her movement grow into a kind of dance, slowly, back and forth before the mirror, in time to her music, *I am so glad*, moving this way and that, tentatively, watching what the movements did...*loves e – ven me*, and then lifting. And waving. Stirring her arms like the wings of a great feathered bird, up and down, *e – ven me*, up and down, *e – ven me*, ever so slowly, her limbs as lithe and gracious as her body, waving

What?

Footsteps? Was it?

Lucille?

Oh, no, her mother's voice, maybe halfway up the stairs already: "Are you still in the bathtub, Marcella?"

Coming! Footsteps clicking off the steps. Robe! Robe! In a heap, on the floor, beside her, snatching it. Arm. Arm. No, the footsteps the. Which arm in the which arm in the oh, no time *now* to get it on *backwards* no! In the hall. She's in the yes. Left arm in, yes, in the hallway, hand on the, right arm in, "No, I'm in here, mother," but too late, grappling with the top buttons, already the door, swinging, oh buttoned *wrong*, never mind, bottom buttons, where she'd have to leave them, and her robe, still swinging *open* when her mother, coming through the door

"What are you doing in here?"

Her words pierced Marcella. She clutched her robe close, flushed under the gaze, her voice, all in a cluster in her throat, oh, she must have tempted the Devil, yes, standing, looking in mirrors, vanity, vanity, all is vanity, sayeth the Lord, if she hadn't *tempted*, she wouldn't be, now, but must say something, say something *anything* oh! Her robe still half-buttoned *open*, part of her breast showing no! fumbling to close it, finding, somewhere, in her stomach, maybe, her voice, it sounded so funny. "Uh. Looking for. Something. Ahhh. Some. Deodorant." So strange sounding, her voice, her mother must *know* she's lying, face all hot and quivering words, "I thought I left it in here." There, the quiver, going, finally going, but her voice, how *loud* getting, careful! careful! she may think I'm talking back, back talk, she hates back talk, and how, father says? Impertinence. "Saw it," there, voice softer. Good. "I thought, I mean, I'd seen it in here, I mean, on your" (looking) "dresser" (stammering) "you know, *vanity*, I mean, not dresser" (turning) "I was just" (reaching) "looking for it" (scrambling through the cluster of glass bottles on the vanity top).

"What do you need deodorant for. It's not Sunday." Staring. Right at her.

"And next time—do button that robe, Marcella—leave the door open, unless you want people to think you are doing something you shouldn't be."

OH! Turning! Oh! How *could* she, none of her *business* what I'm doing in here, none of her –

"ALL RIGHT!" Strong as a curse (God, please forgive) said like that, never mind, refusing to stand, helpless, button robe in front of those, eyes, staring, and it's none of her—oh, I'm going to, absolutely, yes!

Stalking by Mrs. Colby, without so much as an excuse, down the hall, yes! safe to her room, fast, before her mother could even, and what were you doing in my room anyway…

Mrs. Colby started after Marcella. Such impertinence, really, the child is getting to be too much to bear, first that awful slip, and then the religious conversion, oh, my, and hadn't Marcella gotten on her high horse about that, quoting scripture to us all, trying to convert Lucille, at least she'd stopping running around with that awful Cheryl. Now *this*, that deodorant story doesn't fool me any—but she stopped herself in time. Typical, she thought. Typical adolescent behavior. There is no denying it, it is beginning, mercy on us, and probably will be as rugged an adolescence as her childhood has been, grief! Spare us! Babies into children, and then, as soon as you get yourself adjusted to that, off they go…growing into

5

Saved! *O blessed word, how sweet the sound...*it was like a hymn, rising in her, oh! It was like a hymn, its bell-tone chimes reverberating in her ears, its melody lapping around her heart, its deep organ tones bellowing out a song of praise in her very depths. Saved! She had heard her mother complaining, her father, laughing, about her conversion. Marcella didn't care. It was...incredible. Someone to love her, really love her, at last. *I am so glad that our Fa – ther in heaven,* it was like that: voices rising in a joyous song.

Sometimes she could hear it all day long. Some days. If she woke in the right spirit, like she had today, *my heart a – wak – ing cries,* and if she remembered to praise God, "thank you, dear heavenly Father, for the delicious sleep." It made up for having no friends. Then, if she didn't think about Cheryl's little egg jokes, or get mad at Lucille...sun streaming in through her window curtain, "thank you God, for the sun"... then she could sustain it.

She stretched. *Won – der – ful things in the Bi – ble I see; This is the dear – est, that Je – sus loves me. I am so glad...*she was so glad, glad to be waking, glad to have God wake her with his Sun, as He had, before, with His other Son, glad to slide out from under cool percale sheets.

She clambered out of bed.

Now, where were her pants, oh, yes, on the chair. No. Where had they gone? Certain she'd laid them out the night before, right there, on top of the pile, because you put panties on first. Oh, no! Lucille! Of course, she'd taken them, taken her Sunday pants, her favorite in the whole world...that little sneak? Creeping in here in the middle of the night just so she could oh boy, oh boy, wait until I get my hands on

No! On the floor, they must have fallen!

"Oh, Father! Forgive me, for I didn't know..."

It was leaving; she could feel it, receding, the sunlight slipping away from her soul, the lightness seeping from her heart, no! "Please, dear God, please let it stay"...maybe? Oh, how fast it goes! How could it? Leaving her alone, no one to turn to. All her fault, the day scarcely begun, and already sinning! Anger! Vile thoughts! Oh, unhappy day, and she had *promised*.

She tried singing. *I come to the gar - den a - lone, While the dew is still...*"Oh, Father, forgive!" Was He listening? How could she let her heart harden so? *And the voice I hear*—but the words stuck in her throat.

She tried praying. She dropped to her knees, and prayed and prayed until, finally, with her eyes squinched shut, she could begin to see Him—Lucille didn't believe her, but it was true, she could see Him—standing there, in the Garden, the beautiful, beautiful Garden, each leaf waxed green, He in His white robe, looking like He had on Ascension Day, rising on clouds as billowy as the dust storm clouds that sweep the prairie dry, except white and puffy like rain clouds, there He was, but so sad! so so sad His face to see His little one..."I didn't mean it, really I didn't"... walking forward now, beckoning.

And He walks with me, and He talks with me—oh, yes, and it will be All Right, it's going to be All Right, she could almost hear His voice, I am His own.

She could hear Him: MARCELLA, BELOVED OF GOD, YOU ARE FORGIVEN. GO, AND SIN NO MORE. *And He tells me I am His own!*

It was returning, the sunshine, out from behind the sin cloud, returning, the sunshine of His face, His holy face, falling, like fresh rain from the sky, like sun-rain from His radiant face to hers..."Leaving? Already?"

*And the joy we share as we tar – ry there...*so blessed, so willing to forgive, how could she, how dare she sin, after all He'd done for her, how dare she...*as we tar – ry there...*sin against her only begotten divine Father maker of the universe master and lover of all mankind *None oth – er* who was conceived by the Holy Spirit born *has ev – er* of the Virgin Mary *known.*

Whew! What a close one! She rose, shaking her head.

There were only two ways to get it back, after she lost it. Singing, or praying. But sometimes the singing didn't work, because of the Fucks, and the way they might jump into the song.

She slipped into her pants, right foot, left foot. So precious, that feeling, yes, so much so. The only thing that could make up for having no friends, for being so lonely, at school, at home, no one to talk to, not even Lucille. But the sunshine feeling could disappear in the twinkling of an eye. When it did... well, sometimes forgiveness came slower than other times. She pulled her T-shirt over her head. Depending on the sin— so many different kids of sin, and each kind meant a different wrath from God, and a different wait before forgiveness. So difficult, being a Christian.

But she was lucky. So far all her sins had been little ones, sins of o-mission, when you don't do something good, and God forgives that kind pretty quickly, because He knows, in His infinite mercy, that we are weaker than He is, and that nobody in the whole world can live without sinning that sort of sin. But the sin of *com* – mission, that kind is really terrible, that is when you do something bad, on purpose, like taking a drink, or murdering your brother, or coveting your neighbor's ox!

She finished dressing, and found her shoes and socks under the bed.

Like the other day, in the bedroom, before the mirror, not even thinking, in her anger, just blurting "ALL RIGHT!" and storming out of the room. Boy, was she scared that might be a sin of commission, she lost the God feeling for nearly a whole day. She couldn't afford to lose it—if God didn't love her, who would? A good thing she hadn't shouted on purpose, or no telling when He, in His mercy, would return.

And the joy we share when we tar – ry there…

She tied the laces of her oxfords, and—first remembering to read the day's Bible verse from July's *The Upper Room*—went downstairs to breakfast.

6

She had to face it, that's all. She could no longer postpone buying Marcella—a brassiere. She had been hoping that the matter could rest until fall, become part of going-back-to-school clothes, but there could be no more waiting. Marcella's breasts were definitely showing: this morning, at breakfast, her nipples sticking right out over her dish of Corn Flakes, looking like buttons on her T-shirt! Positively disconcerting. And rippling away under her shirt when she ran, just like a chippy's! That undershirt wasn't enough to hold them down. Of course (and Mrs. Colby had to chuckle), Marcella wasn't really *developed* yet, her bust more like the superfluous flesh of a fat boy than like a woman's chest. Still.

She called her daughter in from the yard—probably up in that tree house again, whatever did she find to do up there?

"Go upstairs and get undressed," Mrs. Colby told her. "I need to take some measurements."

"I'll get Lucille," Marcella said. "She's over at the Cronins'."

"Never mind Lucille. This is for something you need. Go along. I'll be right up, as soon as I get the tape measure."

When Mrs. Colby entered the bedroom, minutes later, quilted sewing box in hand, she found Marcella still standing there, in her shirt and blue jeans.

"You're not even undressed! What were you doing, daydream-
ing again?"

Marcella hung her head and wiggled a foot around, disgusting
habit, made her look so sullen. She finally asked:

"In front of you?"

"Goodness, yes, in front of me. I'm not your father."

Mrs. Colby watched Marcella turn her back. So sensitive, all of
a sudden. Like that day in the bedroom, Marcella standing with
robe half unbuttoned, stuttering and stammering like a three-
year-old with wet pants. What did she have to hide? Nothing yet,
that's for sure. Who did she think changed her diapers for her
anyway? Hers, and Lucille's, and, God willing, no more!

Mrs. Colby took the tape from a side pocket of the sewing box,
and looked up to see Marcella's undershirt going over her head.

"No, no! Not your undershirt. I'm only going to take
measurements."

"Oh," Marcella's voice half-smothered as she pulled the shirt
down again. "I thought you meant…" turning around. Standing
once more in undershirt and cotton briefs. Mrs. Colby shook
her head.

"Here. Come over here…That's right. Now lift your arms."
What a piece of wood, this child! "No, no. Lift them. Up, up, up.
High! In the air!" Marcella inched them up a bit farther, then
stopped, her elbows protruding like chicken wings.

"I've got hair under there," she whispered.

So that's what was bothering her.

"Of course you have hair under there." Mrs. Colby flipped the
tape under the girl's arms—"Now lift!"—and pulled it around to
the back. "Do you think you're the only person in the world to
grow hair? Turn around."

Marcella turned, silently. Mrs. Colby matched the tape in
the middle of her back and noted it: only thirty-one. Strange.

Smaller than she'd expected. She leaned forward. Of course! The tape wasn't even across the "full part of the bosom," as they say. She reached to adjust it. Marcella jerked away.

"Stand still, won't you!" Mrs. Colby's voice began to rasp.

"But it tickles!"

"Oh, don't be so silly. Here, turn and face me, then. I have to get the measurement across your chest. It does no good if the tape is lying across your belly."

Mrs. Colby pulled the tape around, or tried to. Marcella kept squirming, jerking each time her mother's hand grazed her breast.

"My! Aren't you something! How do you expect me to get an accurate measurement, if you keep shifting around all the time? You must stay still, Marcella. And stand up straight. How can I tell a thing with your shoulders all hunched over like that?"

"Let me do it. Here." Marcella grabbed the tape. "Where does it go?"

"That's right," watching her lay the yellow-and-red tape gently, first across one undershirted nipple, then across the other. "Now let me have it," Mrs. Colby pulled the tape together in front of Marcella's armpit, so she could see the "full parts" without accidentally touching them. "Now put your arms down. Stand nice and straight." She squinted front and back: tape across nipples, tape in flat line across shoulder blades, not riding too high, nor too low. "Stand still."

"You're pulling it too tight."

"Nonsense." But she released the tape a little. "Mmmmmmm. Thirty-two and a half. Call it thirty-two." She flipped the tape away.

"But it wasn't comfortable."

"You're not used to the way it feels, that's all," with a deft flick calculating the five and a half inches below the waist to get a perfect hip measurement, the tape down and around the tiny buttocks, above their swelling, across the widespread pelvic bones. Thirty-four.

So her measurements hadn't changed that much at all, must be the shifting in shape that made her seem different.

"You can get dressed now," Mrs. Colby said.

Gladys Harding ran, without doubt, the most popular dress shop in Hildreth, sandwiched right between the Ben Franklin Five-and-Dime and Jake's Liquor Store. They said her shop did more business of a weekend than the big J. C. Penney store over in Phelpsburg, a town almost twice the size of Hildreth. Of course, Mrs. Colby couldn't say about that. J. C. Penney was considerably cheaper than Gladys's shop (for that matter, so was ordering from the Sears catalog) but for some things…well, Gladys had what you might call a "personal" touch. Going to her store was more like stopping by for coffee with a friend than shopping.

"It's for Marcella," Mrs. Colby confided, after she and the shop owner had discussed the health of both families, and exchanged the latest church news. "She's beginning to develop—already!"

"Fancy," Mrs. Harding replied, leading the way to her lingerie counter. "They certainly do grow up fast, don't they? What size?"

"Don't they ever! I guess a thirty-two. She measured only a fraction over. But I've no idea what size cup."

"A," Mrs. Harding nodded emphatically. "Try an A."

"Oh goodness, Gladys!" Mrs. Colby laughed. "She'll never fill out an A. I mean, she's developing, all right, but she isn't exactly bursting through her clothes."

"Sort of at that awkward stage?"

"Yes. I even tried covering them with an undershirt, but it isn't enough. Still…don't they make double A's! Or better yet, triple?"

"You're thinking of shoes, Lois." Mrs. Harding was laughing, too. "They come as small as five-A, now."

"Exactly what she needs—thirty-two-AAAAA! It would fit her perfectly! Oh, my, Gladys," wiping tears from her eyes, "they do come small at the beginning, don't they."

"We could special order an extra-small brassiere from Munsingwear, they put out a junior line. But if she's that small, Lois, why bother? It's not the undergarments that make the girls conspicuous, I say, it's how you dress them. Like that Shurf girl. The one whose folks just bought the old Mantz place over south of town?"

Mrs. Colby knew them. All the Shurfs were Methodists.

"Now she is what I call fully developed—really, Lois, she and her mother came in the other day, and if you could see the girl. Every bit as full as you or me. But you'd never notice, the way Mrs. Shurf dressed her in those bibbed yokes and shirred bodices and—just between us, she buys them a size too big, so they won't pull. Covers that girl right up! And I mean that child's better developed than the Dietz girl...I don't gossip, you know me, Lois, but that Ella Dietz. Surely no one in town hasn't noticed her, acting like a hussy with those tight T-shirts, and those low-cut blouses..."

"Oh, it's shameful! How can her mother let her carry on that way. Someone should talk to her."

"You'd think she could see it herself, don't you? Plain enough to most people. But T-shirts are such a fad this year, the girls think they have to wear them. Strutting down the street, advertising everything they've got—I don't know. They don't leave much to the imagination, do they?"

Mrs. Colby nodded agreement, dreading trouble to come— Marcella wearing lipstick, Marcella out chasing boys, running with a fast crowd, acting cheap. And Lucille right on her heels. Oh, raising girls is so complicated!

"Well, there's no use arguing," continued Mrs. Harding. "Children get so stubborn at that age. But buying shirts too large, that's a good trick, and so is this." She walked briskly to the end of the counter, and held up a brightly striped T-shirt. "Have you seen these, Lois? The stripes are such a blessing. You can hardly see the—if you'll excuse the expression—nipple marks. Of course, you're the judge. Maybe a bra would be better…"

Mrs. Colby considered. Marcella's breasts not much bigger than a pair of onions, really, but they do protrude. Not even the extra undershirt is enough to camouflage them.

"No, Gladys, I'd better stick to the brassiere. Otherwise, I'll just be running down here next month. There's no postponing adolescence."

Mrs. Harding inclined her head, and trotted back down the counter aisle, reaching into a stack of blue-and-white boxes to pull out several thirty-two-A samples.

"We can always special order the Munsingwear Junior if the thirty-two-A is too large. But here, let me show you Kayser's 'starter bra.' It's really quite clever." She folded back the tissue paper and lifted the brassiere, turning the cup inside out. "See how they've made this with quilting along the cup sides? Junior Foundettes, they call them. Now thirty-two-A is the outside measurement, really. The padding makes it considerably smaller, so a girl who actually fills an A cup find it a bit snug."

"Oh, but Gladys, certainly Marcella's too young for padding."

"Yes, of course, but this isn't padding in the usual sense of the word. It's more like filler. If you get a thirty-two-A without quilting, she may not be able to fill it out herself, you know, and if she can't, the cup will crumple back on her chest. Well, I don't have to tell you how that looks. And another thing. The quilting covers up so much better. It even conceals the, pardon the expression, nipples—oh, so much better than your regular brassiere."

That settled it. Mrs. Colby looked at some other styles, but in the end, after selecting a garter belt and stockings, she bought the quilted brassiere. In fact, she bought two.

It took a while for Mrs. Colby to figure out how to introduce the clothes to Marcella. For that was her idea, to introduce them, to make them seem important. It could be a critical step in the process of transforming her daughter into a lady. To woo her away from any ideas she might have of becoming a hussy, a common pickup. Oh, girls! She knew how their minds ran with pretty things, lacy things. These matters were so delicate...how to create the proper atmosphere, making the privilege of wearing grown-up things acquire its own code, its duties. For she would have to direct Marcella, somehow, that was clear. But not too bluntly. No, not outright. If there was one thing she understood about her daughter, it was Marcella's stubbornness. Tell her she had to do something, and she'd end up doing the opposite. Oh, a delicate matter indeed.

She waited until after lunch, having made arrangements for Lucille to visit a friend. That way, she and Marcella wouldn't be interrupted. She called her daughter into the bedroom.

"What's this?" Marcella wanted to know, as Mrs. Colby gave her the store-wrapped packages.

"The clothes I measured you for. Go ahead. Open them up."

Marcella pulled a tangle of elastic and ribbon out of the first package. The ribbons were attached to a piece of smooth white satin, a rose embroidered in one corner.

"Oh," she cried, "for me?" As silky as Rosemary's slip!

"Yes, but here. Try this one first," and Mrs. Colby set the flat hose box aside, to hand her daughter the third box. Inside, under folds of tissue, Marcella found another scramble of straps, hooks and eyes, and delicate edgings. These weren't silky though. Just cotton. Quilted cotton.

"Is it…" Marcella couldn't bring herself to say the word in front of her mother.

"A brassiere," Mrs. Colby replied as matter of factly as she could, unscrambling the straps. "Two of them. Here. Let me help you." She stripped Marcella's T-shirt and undershirt off in one swift motion, before the girl had time to be shy.

"Mother! Really! I can take off my own clothes."

"Did I catch your nose? Sorry."

Mrs. Colby picked up the brassiere.

"No! Here. Let me!" Marcella insisted. She took the brassiere and stuck her arms through the strap holes, as though she were donning a coat. Then, reconsidering, she turned it around so the breast pieces were in front.

"Not that way. You've got it upside down." Mrs. Colby deftly retrieved the brassiere, circled it around Marcella, pulled the elastic taut, and fastened the hooks in the last row of eyes. Snug! That was strange. She was certain the measurement had been only thirty-two and a half, and Marcella with such little breasts…She twisted the circle of cotton around the girl's body. "There. Now you can put your arms through."

Marcella began wiggling into the cups.

"No, not like that. Bend over." She helped her daughter jiggle her breasts into the quilted containers.

The straps hung in long ribbons off Marcella's shoulders. Mrs. Colby adjusted the bands, pushing the metal clips. "Move around a bit and see how it feels."

It felt awkward. The elastic dug into Marcella's chest; the padded cups pushed her breasts flat against her body.

"I don't know," said Marcella. "I can barely move."

"Well, there's no call to move. It's not good for your bosom to jiggle all over the place."

"It's pretty tight."

"Why don't you wear it awhile, and see. We can always exchange it. But better too small than too big—that elastic stretches with washing, anyway. Besides, I think you'll be more comfortable with a snug fit, once you get used to it. When you run, especially. Come. Let's see how it looks under your T-shirt."

"Shouldn't I put my undershirt on first?" She'd been wearing them all summer long, even on the hottest days—every since her breasts became noticeable.

"Oh, no. You wear this instead of an undershirt."

"Every day?" Marcella was incredulous. She had thought maybe on Sundays, maybe with dresses...

"Yes, every day. Of course. That's why I bought two. Here. Put your t-shirt on."

Marcella's voice came muffled through her shirt:

"You mean Rosemary wears a bra every day?"

"Well, if she doesn't, she should," Mrs. Colby sniffed, watching the cups ride up on Marcella's breasts as she wriggled into the shirt. "And say 'brassiere,' Marcella. 'Bra' is vulgar. Here. Don't wiggle so much." She helped her daughter jounce her breasts back into the cups again. The brassiere was too tight, there was no mistaking it. Cups too small! But how could she return it, after...

"There. Let's see how you look." Oh, Gladys was right! No sign of nipple marks, only the cross-stitching at the tip of the cup. Although the bosom, well, actually the breasts did protrude, but they seemed... "Move around a bit, Marcella, and let me have a look." Excellent! Her breasts remained as static as marble ones. With a larger T-shirt, maybe striped...infinitely better.

Marcella stood staring at her breasts. They seemed too gigantic. She seemed all breasts, nothing but these huge lumps slapped on her chest, oh! Every day! She would surely get teased. How awful Rosemary must feel, with hers so big. You had to peek over the points to see your own feet! No longer flat, like a child, and wearing undershirts, but stuck with this contraption all the time, ugh! How could she even run, any more, the elastic cutting in every which way, and hot! Whew! All this quilting, hotter than her undershirt had been, and pushing her breasts so tightly against her, they felt like an enormous ledge, a slab of flesh and cotton bound to her chest.

"And you let the other one air out the next day," her mother was explaining. "that way, they don't get smelly."

"Don't you wash them?"

"On Saturdays, with the rest of the clothes. Not by hand, that's too much bother. See what else I got you?"

Mrs. Colby held up the garter belt. Marcella was alarmed.

"Do I have to wear that every day, too?"

"Goodness, no. This is only for Sundays. To hold up your hose."

Marcella knew what the belt was for, but it looked suspiciously confining…though it was pretty. She took it, and began smoothing the satin part. So grown-up. As pretty as that slip had been. Maybe it wouldn't be so bad, and only for dress-up…

"…like a lady," her mother was saying. "Don't ever let me catch you sitting like this." Marcella looked. Mrs. Colby sat on the edge of her bed, knees flung apart, toes turned in. "Anybody can see right up your skirt if you sit like this." The thought was startling. Then Mrs. Colby crossed her legs, letting one foot dangle in the air. "And don't this this way, either.

"Crossing legs is okay for older women, like myself," she explained, "but not for young girls. They just look fast. Besides, it's a good way to snag your hose with the heel of your shoe. You can cross your ankles, if you must. But here's how a nice girl sits."

So strange to have to show Marcella all this. Lucille just seemed to know—or was it that she was a better mimic? Anyway…

"Now you try it." Mrs. Colby pointed to her dressing table stool. "Legs together, fleet flat." No daughter of here would become a hussy, like Ella Dietz, or like that Cheryl Riker, for that matter. "Keep those knees together. That's better. There's that's perfect! Shall we try the belt, now?"

Marcella nodded.

"Here. No, no. The other way. It goes on just like the brassiere did." Fastening the hook in the middle loop, at least this fit right, and twisting the belt around Marcella's pants, pulling around underneath it, cut into her leg. Mrs. Colby helped her to get untangled.

"You usually wear it under your panties, of course, though some women like to wear it over theirs, so the seams won't leave marks, but that's a bother. You have to take everything down every time you go to the bathroom. There."

The white satin inset lay flat against Marcella's stomach, the red rose floating above a hip bone. "Oh," she smoothed it down. "It's so pretty." *Meet me in St. Lou – ee, Lou – ee.* And white. Like Ginger Roger's wedding garter! Wait until Lucille sees this!

"Leave the straps longer in the back," Mrs. Colby advised, "so they give a little when you sit down." She held out the last package. Marcella ripped the paper off.

"Oh!" Not believing it. "Real rayons? Real rayons, mother?"

"Yes, but only for Sundays, of course. And special occasions. They're not toys, you know."

Marcella was afraid to touch them, lying so sheer and flat in the box, looking every bit as fragile and shimmery as the forbidden silk hose she and Cheryl had tried on. Before she was saved, of course. She lifted them out of the box. The stockings held their strange flat shapes as though they were starched. Mrs. Colby had chosen a simple pair—no embroidery, no sequins, not even black seams or outlined heels. Only simple brown heels giving way to long brown seams.

"You'll have to treat them carefully. They're not cheap. Of course, it's not as if they were silk, but still, they cost enough. If you treat them properly, they should last a good while."

Treating them properly meant not snagging them. And washing them right, letting them dry for two days, because if you didn't, you might as well wear them once and throw them away.

"Real rayons," Marcella said. She could hardly wait to try them on, to feel that sheer material on her legs. Wouldn't Cheryl be green! Oh! She wished she could show her.

Her mother was still talking. Not snagging them meant, first, keeping your toenails clipped (Mrs. Colby handed her the clippers, and she trimmed, while her mother talked) and, next, watching where you are going, and last, sitting like a proper lady so the hose doesn't catch on chair rungs, or your shoes.

Finally, it was time to put them on.

Mrs. Colby fetched a pair of thin summer gloves from her dresser drawer. "Just a precaution," she said, pulling the gloves on, "but a good one to cultivate. The gloves serve as protection, so a fingernail, or a hangnail—you can't be too careful—doesn't catch in them." The ruffled cuffs of the gloves stood up like Elizabethan collars around her wrists. "Sometimes I don't bother, but I think you should, especially at first."

Marcella watched her roll the stocking all the way down to its ankle, like old Mrs. Schneider next door wore her everyday hose in the summertime, rolled like brown doughnuts around her ankles.

"Now, then, don't shove your foot in. Here. Point your toe, that's right, like a ballerina, and ever so gently lift—see how I'm doing it?—the rayon over your foot."

"Oh," Marcella breathed out, watching the stocking turn the skin of her tanned feet still a shade darker. Mrs. Colby carefully positioned the heel—"Now put your foot down"—and lifted the stocking all the way to the knee. *Ni – ta, Jua – a – a – ni – ta!* The rayon flattened Marcella's hair against her leg, the hair made strange patterns through the sheer web, the web so cool against her skin—my, she was really sweating! Even her thighs were damp. *Tell the world...*

"Did you notice," asked her mother, "the way I used my thumbs to guide the seam?" She rolled the stocking down once more, once more lifted it up, using her thumbs to guide seams dead center up the back of Marcella's leg. "You'll get to know when it feels straight, after a while," she explained, guiding not so carefully up the thighs, because no one sees your thighs anyway, not if you are a nice girl, so the thigh seam can be a little crooked. Not too crooked, of course, or it will throw the rest of the seam off, all the way down to the ankle.

Mrs. Colby supervised the donning of the second stocking closely—"Not too loose. It will wrinkle at the ankle." The clips were a cinch. All you had to remember was not to clip on the sheer part, to adjust the straps tightly, but not too tightly (in case you had to bend over), and to put the back clips on the outsides of your legs so the straps slide out, not in, when you sit. Oh! The stockings were delicious, so delicate—and so warm! How could such flimsy things be so hot? But their silkiness! Marcella wished her mother weren't here so she could run her bare hands up and down her legs, just to *feel* them. *And the way they shake.*

The hose made her legs as brown and shiny as her mother's floor. But sitting down—she must have fastened the garter belt wrong, somehow, because when she sat, the whole complicated rigging shifted alarmingly around, the front straps going loose and buckling, the back straps pulling ever so tight, the weight pulling the whole belt down into her soft buttocks.

"Is this right?"

"Mmmmmm," said Mrs. Colby, inspecting. "It looks just fine."

Marcella went to the full-length mirror. Mrs. Colby taught her how to check her seams by twisting so she could look over her shoulder into the mirror. Then she showed Marcella how to straighten the seam, not by tugging, but by grasping her whole leg with both hands, and gently rotating the rayon. "If you tug, you'll snap them."

Bending over, the belt gouged unexpectedly at Marcella's stomach. It pinched even worse than the brassiere. Obviously, you had to move cautiously with these things on. Straightening, she caught sight of her mother's flat wrinkle-free stomach and, pointing at it, asked:

"When do I have to start wearing those?"

"Girdles?"

Marcella nodded. Her mother never went without hers, no matter how stifling hot the day.

"Oh, goodness, child," Mrs. Colby tried not to laugh. "Not for a while. Not until you get old, and flabby, from having kids, like me. Now then. Let's see you. Don't you look fancy! Straighten up, and throw your shoulders back. That's better. Oh, my, what a nice lady you're going to be!"

Watching her daughter examine her shiny new legs in the mirror, Mrs. Colby figured out what she would do about the two-tight brassieres. She wouldn't return them, after all. No. She'd simply splice a piece of elastic in the back of each one. Those small cups should hold Marcella's breasts down better anyway. There must be extra elastic around somewhere.

"Leave that brassiere on, Marcella, until I get the other one fixed." She put the lid of her sewing box. "And take those hose off now. But do be careful. Don't ruin them."

She headed downstairs toward the sewing machine. My! How much she'd accomplished this day.

7

One sweltering evening, early in August, after listening to the news and the "Amos 'n' Andy" show, Mr. Colby wandered out the kitchen door to plop himself on the old wooden porch swing. Marcella saw him go. It was Wednesday. On Mondays, he listened to Gracie Allen, and on Tuesdays, to "Fibber McGee and Molly," and on Wednesdays, after "Amos 'n' Andy"…well, she wasn't going to get trapped out there, swinging back and forth in the sultry prairie night, pretending to laugh at his tales. She stalled, putting dishes away slower and slower, until she saw Lucille leave, and heard the porch swing creak to a stop, and start again, voices rising, soft and full.

By the time Marcella headed out the front door and circled the house, Mr. Colby was already hard at it: "'Member the time I scared your poor mother plumb out of her mind?" he was asking Lucille. "The time she thought I'd chopped my thumb clean off?" And he was retelling it—once more—how he'd come running in the back door, groaning and whinnying, handkerchief covering the edge of the rubber thumb he'd bought at the Ben Franklin store, the thumb swollen twice as big as his real one, and purple, ketchup dripping off his hand like blood. "Hoooooo, hoooooo, hoooooo! You should of seen her face," he wheezed, creaking the swing back and forth. "I thought she'd pass dead away! Hooooo, hooooo."

Down below them, on the steps, Marcella sat—safe! She could hear what he said without having to respond, she could just sit, watching the shadows of the sullen night, and listen—or half-listen—to his talk. That was okay. She noted the night sounds: heels clicking hollowly on some distant sidewalk, voices as wispy as cobwebs, trapped in the heavy night, and the hoarse cro – ak, cro – ak of far-off frogs. And beyond the town, the prairie. She could almost hear it rattling a faint chorus of snakes and weeds.

"Come on up here with us city folk," Mr. Colby hollered down at her, but Marcella wouldn't budge. "Getting as stuck-up as her mother," he told Lucille in a loud voice. "Thinks she's too good for us, huh."

Marcella didn't reply. She'd given up trying to explain to him, he always took everything wrong, and anyway, how could she tell him why she wouldn't sit on the swing any more? He'd only laugh if she said she was getting too old for that now, but she was, she was almost thirteen, that was too old to share the swing with him, laugh at his jokes, squeal when he grabbed a fist full of hair or stuck an unexpected finger in her ribs. How could she explain? She no longer felt comfortable there, especially now she was wearing a brassiere and everything, it made her uneasy: the heat of her father's arm running along the swing back, the weight of his hand dropping down on her head, as heavy as the air before a tornado.

Besides, he kept teasing her. Only last week, bringing home catfish from the murky river waters, their spiny whiskers still twitching. She watched him splitting the white belly skin open, as neat and clean as slicing the white of a hard-boiled egg, dipping his fingers inside, lifting out clusters of orange beads, as translucent as vitamin pills—eggs! "Here, this one's dead, go ahead, stick your finger in its mouth and see." But it wasn't dead, it bit her; how he laughed…She didn't trust him. Well, there. So what. It was true. He had led her on one time too many, with his jokes about putting salt on a robin's tail, and catching Santa Claus, and trapping the Easter Bunny. He even brought home Mexican jumping beans, held races, and bet on them. She lost her whole allowance.

Let Lucille fall for his tricks. Lucille could still believe him, she was only a kid, not even eleven yet. What was the use of it, anyway, crying yourself to sleep thinking Santa Claus wasn't coming, just so *he* could laugh at your surprised face the next morning.

"Well, pet, one day Ray, your Uncle Ray, remember him? The one with the farm over by the Old Place? He was lipping off more than was good for him, so we just up and tied him to the arms of the old windmill. Yes, sir. Spread-eagled him like a big X and let him ride! Hoooo, hoooo—and wouldn't you know it, this breeze springs up and Ray, he commences spinning around, pale as a ghost. 'You scared, Ray?' we hollered, but he didn't answer none, just shook his head once when he slowed down. So we left him up there until after sundown. Saved him a plate of food from supper, but he didn't eat none. Said he wasn't hungry! Hooooo! Hoooooo! I reckon he was too darned dizzy to eat, yes, sir, but he would deny it. That's your Uncle Ray, all right, 'Nope, dizzy? Nope, not me,' and could barely stand upright, reeling along like a three-legged pig on ice skates!"

Mr. Colby laughing, elbowing Lucille, Lucille giggling along with him, the back-porch swing creaking, and a pale moon starting to show through the black branches of the elm trees.

"Well, that's a Colby for you. Not one of them would ever admit they was scared. Not one. 'Mighty fine sunset you lads showed me,' that's all old Ray ever said about it."

"Tell me the one about the electric shock," Lucille was begging, she knew how to please him, all right, and Mr. Colby nodding his head, getting ready to spin the tale about Uncle Ike and Uncle Pete, studying electricity in the one-room schoolhouse where all the Colbys, brothers and cousins, had gone.

But Marcella didn't stay to hear the story. She couldn't stand hearing that laugh again, his laughter was setting her teeth on edge, and besides, she knew what came next. Next he would sit and swing a bit, and then he'd send Lucille off to bed—"You'd better scoot now, before that mother of yours beats me up for letting you stay out so late"—and he'd kiss her, and tousle her hair, and pop a "love pat" on her behind before he sent her away.

It was awful, that kissing business. Sometimes he would grab Marcella and hug her so tight she couldn't even breathe! And he never would let go until he was good and ready, just laughing, like it was a game. Sometimes she tried to pull away, but his arms were so strong she couldn't, oh! And then he'd whisker her, his black rough stubble grating her cheek and raising tears in her eyes, his breath all stale from cigarettes, or worse, if he'd been out playing cards. Terrible.

She cut out, slipping quietly off the steps so he wouldn't notice, running fast through the silent dark spaces at the side of the house, fast, around the corner and up the front steps before you could recite Jack Sprat.

8

Marcella tried to convince herself that it was *not* a sin of commission. It was all Cheryl's fault, anyway. If she hadn't met Cheryl coming home from the library, if she hadn't started walking side-by-side with her like they used to after school, down the curbstone, if she had gone straight home, instead, then it never would have happened. Oh, why hadn't she listened to her mother: "There are so many nice girls in your class. Why do you insist on running around with that Cheryl Riker?"

Her mother was right. Cheryl's house so different from theirs, so dim, the wallpaper peeling, stuff scattered all around. She'd never thought much of it before. Of course, Cheryl's mom didn't have a chance to keep the place clean, always out waiting tables and so many kids to mess things up: Rosemary, the two older boys, Cheryl and Lynn, and little Alvin with his flaming red hair. So many. And some kids said that Cheryl's mother let Cheryl's father do funny stuff to her all the time, and that's why she had so many children, and where did she get a red-headed boy anyway, so maybe she let other men do it, too.

Like Rosemary.

Rosemary let boys do things to her, even Karen Harding said so, and once she let a man—everybody knew it, how a man had taken Rosemary into the piney woods behind the power plant and had *done* things to her, maybe even touched her, so that nobody was supposed to speak to her, or to Cheryl, or to any of the Riker kids any more. And nobody did, after that, not for a whole month, not even Marcella, and Cheryl had been her best friend in the whole world, but that didn't matter.

They still weren't speaking, not very often, anyway, not since her conversion, and if she hadn't forgotten herself and started walking along the curbstones with Cheryl like nothing had happened, then she never would have...oh! If only! Or if only they'd gone straight home, and not stopped by...but they stopped. They stopped on the sidewalk in front of the white frame Catholic Church, and Cheryl said, "Come on. I have to go inside and light a candle."

It made Marcella's back chilly, hearing her.

"What for?"

"For grandpa," Cheryl said. "He died, oh, almost a year ago. Mom said I had to."

Standing on the sidewalk, the sun so hot on the back of her neck, the shivers going down her arm, what was in there, anyway? Waiting? Priests, the kids say, who hang around casting spells on everyone, and statues, yes, even though the First Commandment says no other gods before me, and heathen things. And the priests hide in black boxes and make crosses over you when you're not looking and...

If Cheryl's grandfather hadn't been dead, they never would have gone inside.

"I'll wait out here," Marcella said, and she would have, but Cheryl laughed at her.

"Scaredy-cat," she said. "There's nobody in there, except maybe some old lady praying. There's never anybody in there on weekdays. Come on."

It was a sin of pride, it was. She didn't want Cheryl to think she was chicken, not Marcella, not a Colby, so she said: "Pooh. I'm not scared. But I'm not supposed to go in there, you know that."

"Well, I won't tell. So nobody will ever know. Besides, it's too hot to wait out here. It'll be cool inside. Come on."

Cheryl turned and skipped up the front steps. Marcella followed. And *that* wasn't Cheryl's fault, not really, only maybe a little bit because she talked her into it. But Marcella had decided to go in. So it was a sin of commission, after all, not a sin of omission, even if going inside was only a little sin of commission, not like killing somebody, but more like, more like coveting a neighbor's ox. So that God would have been mad at her, but not like this: she looked around her sick room, at the white sheets, the thermometer, the water glass, the awful sulfa pills that stuck in her throat. She knew.

Her mother thought it was only a sort of heat stroke, at first, anyway—oh, it had been hot that day, walking home, 104° in the shade her father said, but maybe he was kidding. Still, it wasn't the heat...

So cool in the church, and so pretty. That really surprised her. She thought it would be dark, and awful, with maybe even bats flying around, but no. The ceiling was ever so high, and arched. And the walls were blue! Blue as the sky, clear clear blue you could almost see summer clouds scudding by, getting darker and darker, until the walls and ceiling turned a deep night blue around the altar. And the windows, so thinly colored, letting in ever so much light, almost like being outdoors.

The pews, pale oak, and the altars, so light, not like heavy Methodist pews and the dark sad colors there, but so delicate, lace runners on the altars, and flowers, even though it wasn't Sunday, and so many candles. Everywhere you looked, candles, flowers, *something*—it was like a lady, this church, soft and light and delicate and fussy, so full of things, so cluttered, it was, it was—feminine. What a relief. If only she hadn't –

"What are those?" she asked, watching Cheryl cross herself and sort of half kneel. Stations of the Cross, Cheryl said, fourteen of them, carving out the story of Black Friday in different little scenes, each one numbered, so you could follow them.

The girls walked toward the votive candles, piled in their high pyramid, glittering at the altar end of the church, Cheryl, going to light one for her long dead grandfather, maybe pray him from purgatory into heaven, that's what they thought. And that babies go to hell, isn't that awful?

Statues, everywhere, graven images, only Cheryl didn't call them that, but Marcella knew, the minute she looked at them, and she knew she shouldn't look, but she did, just the same: "That's Jesus." Of course it was Jesus, standing there in His graven image with His sacred heart hanging out of His clothes, bloody and red, looking awful, even with the golden cross on it. "St. Joseph," Cheryl continued, pointing, "and St. Anne, mother of Mary. See? She's teaching the young Virgin to read."

Marcella watched Cheryl light a candle, taking the flame from another one, and she watched her drop down on the little kneeling bench to pray. Marcella started to step up on the altar, but held back. "That's okay," Cheryl said, looking up at her. "You can walk anywhere you want to. It doesn't matter."

So if only she had waited there, sitting in a pew and waiting, not walking around or anything, then maybe it wouldn't have happened, but she didn't. She walked up into the altar area and looked: at the tiny bells dangling on the walls, at the big candles, some standing as tall as she, at the huge Bible with bands of colored ribbons hanging out.

It was darker up on the altar than back in the pews, more cave like, everything all shadowed and dusky. She stood before the huge communion table with the Last Supper carved on its front panel. On top, an enormous silver chalice waited, empty. Above, a gigantic cross hung, way down from the ceiling, almost touching the table top, a big gold cross with…there were feet on it!

Backing up, looking up, and *seeing* it. She had never seen a crucifix before, not a big one, only empty crosses, but this was hung with…He was as big as Mr. Colby, He really was, this Jesus, His body brown as clay. Blood, dribbling down His side! *And sin – ers plunged be – neath that flood.* Bolts, real bolts through His feet and through His wrists, not His hands, but stuck right into His arms. More blood, on His head, too, *Thy flow – ing wounds sup – ply* dribbling down His forehead from His crown of thorns, still stuck tight *Dear dy – ing lamb, Thy pre – cious…*

She fought back tears, the desire to pray…it was not meet and right to worship here, that's why you should never come in, because you might mistake and fall down and worship, it would make God furious, oh! *a foun – tain filled* you could not imagine how mad he got when you worshiped those graven images, so she made herself unclench her hands, which had gripped themselves together for a prayer without her really knowing what they were doing.

The tears trickled down her cheeks and onto the pillow. She hadn't let them out, there, in the church, but they were spilling now, *lies si – lent in the grave,* sliding down her cheeks as she remembered the graven image of her beloved Saviour, and the pain, the awful pain He must have gone through…but if she had left, even then, and gone right back out into the sunlight, and never ever looked around any more, even then, she would have committed only the sin of going into the church, like coveting the ox, no more, for she hadn't worshiped there—nearly, but had not, not sinned the worse than Thou shalt not kill sin oh! Her body, flushed with the fever of the sickness that had dropped down upon her almost as soon as she left the church, going back into the hot sunlight, dragging herself home, so reluctantly, home, her chastisement and her repentance warring down the long cement blocks, so she didn't even hear Cheryl chattering, or remember saying goodbye, the fever that He was punishing her with. Her body, flushed, beneath the clean white sheets, began to shake with sobs, silent sobs, for of course her mother must not know, *no one* must know, it was bad enough that God knew… oh, it was her fault, really, hers and hers alone, that's why she was paying for it this way, only…maybe…maybe the priest had put a spell on her, she thought she saw one, as she turned, a sudden flicker of black at the back of the church. But probably it was just the confessional booth with its long black curtains. Or maybe the graven image of a nun, Cheryl showed her, all in black with its fleshy-colored face…maybe that's what she'd seen. Only it had *moved*, she was quite certain it—

"What's that?" Freezing, and whispering, for talking out loud didn't seem right in a sanctuary. Cheryl only laughed, and began leaving, walking down the far aisle.

Marcella followed. She was glad she wasn't going first. Her heart was beating so hard, and she kept straining her eyes to see… maybe it really was a priest and he was still watching them… so that she almost missed the snake. Except she *bumped* it. She bumped the snake, and when she looked down to see what she had bumped, her hand was resting right *on* it—how she jerked away! But it was only a make-believe snake, she saw that, but what if Cheryl had seen her jump? but Cheryl was way ahead, and the snake felt, so cold, to her touch.

Then she saw the foot.

The foot was standing on the snake, the snake all golden and brown and squashed down in the middle from the weight of the foot, he was dying, oh, it must be the snake of the knowledge of good and evil, *dying*—his mouth wide open in his death gasp, his bright white teeth painted in a brilliant pink mouth, in convulsions there...

She let her face tilt up a little to look at, the statue, though somehow, she knew from the beginning who would be there, maybe because of the snake, and maybe because she hadn't seen her yet, the Virgin Mother, and she knew they bowed down and worshiped her, it was one of the most awful things Catholics do, praying to Mary like she was God, but reluctantly up, up, Marcella's eyes went, afraid to confirm it. Up slow miles of rich white folds, up her robe, blue, blue as the sky, blue as the bright church walls, maybe that's why she hadn't noticed her, as light and blue and white as the Church, her robe edged with gold paint. The folds looked so much like cloth, but when Marcella touched them, they were cold, cold as the snake, plaster cold, she could almost smell the plaster, but when she pulled back, and looked...so real, it seemed like Mary was almost *breathing* there.

Her waist was bound round with a golden tasseled rope, how real it was! You could see each tiny cord! And out, out, to her hands, to the delicate white hands, unbroken by nails, she held them, palms open, as though she, not He, were saying, "Suffer the little children to come unto me, and forbid them not: for of such is the kingdom of God." Marcella could almost hear her speaking, knowing how soft and gentle her voice would be, how fragile, as fragile as the white beads that hung, oh, looking like real pearls, not plaster, but beautiful mother-of-pearl beads, her rosary dangling from one hand.

Swiftly, then—for Marcella felt herself about to cry—she looked to the face, what a strange face! gazing down, ever so gently, down at Marcella, more then serene, as though Mary rested beyond all expression, as though nothing meant anything to her, nothing at all, but you, nothing but you, the *eyes* said it. The eyes, they caught hold of you, gaze to gaze, gripping, and the face became, no, not a statue's at all, but...compassion! Such compassion! As though the Blessed Virgin could see right into your soul, as though she had known you forever and ever amen, as though...

What was she *doing*!

Marcella's hand, her own hand, finishing...she must have seen Cheryl doing it...the sign of the cross, what did that mean? And mumbling! She thought she was only thinking the words, only hearing them inside her head, but some of them came right out: "Holy Mary, Mother of God, pray for me, please pray for me..."

What was she doing, *kneeling* there, oh Holy Virgin, oh Jesus Lord, oh dear God forgive me...and hearing Cheryl's voice, "Come on, dopey. Hurry up. What's taking you so long?" So Cheryl must have seen her...

Standing, spotting the slit of sunlight from the open door, bolting, fleeing, past the light oak pews, past the black nun statue, was it moving? Oh Mother of God! Past the blacker than night confessional booth, suppose a *priest* was in there, *looking*, past...oh, dear Jesus, let me reach the door before he can hex me. Out, out, slipping on a step, catching the rail, not safe until...the sidewalk. The sidewalk, a public place, and shaking, she could feel herself shaking from it, her skin still cool from the church, but beads of perspiration rolling down the sides of her head onto her cheek...

"What's the matter," Cheryl saying, "see a spook?" Laughing. Marcella replying: "*Nothing's* the matter. Nothing at all," and sweating, not recognizing her own voice, but it must have been hers because Cheryl believed it, and walking home, all the way home through the hot afternoon sun, and feeling it, dropping down on her, the wrath of God like a black tornado cloud around her, burning with its white-hot summer winds, and ice-cold,

cold as the vacuum of its dead-air center, sweeping her hot and cold in turn, the perspiration streaming, then drying in thin cold lines on her flesh, until, finally, safely home...her mother asking: "What's the matter? You're as pale as a ghost. Here. Let me take your temperature." And *wanting* to, *wanting* to tell—oh, mother, he did hand me the fruit and I did eat—but being oh! (her body was shaking again) finally, unable to speak, it was so awful, what she had done to Him, how could He ever forgive her: *I am the Lord thy God...thou shalt have no other gods before me. Thou shalt not make thee any graven image, or any likeness of anything that is in heaven above, or that is in the earth beneath, or that is in the water beneath the earth: Thou shalt not bow down thyself...* oh what, oh what had she done!

9

She lay in bed sick until the middle of winter. It was not the first time. She had been sick a whole term, a whole school term, once, in third grade, but that had been different. They had known what was the matter then, like they know which germs make measles: a viral infection, they had said, and Mrs. Colby had made Marcella keep up with her schoolwork, but this. She was supposed to be in seventh grade now, but too sick to do homework, at least at first, and nobody knew what was wrong.

Maybe another virus, said Doctor Fisher, and he prescribed the big yellow sulfa pills and lots of rest, but Marcella didn't get better.

They took her from hospital to hospital, in Phelpsburg, and even all the way to Kansas City. One doctor said maybe rheumatic fever, and one said maybe TB, and the last one said he didn't know what was wrong and there was no way to tell. He prescribed rest. Aspirin to keep her fever down. Sulfa to keep the germs away.

The Colbys talked about taking her to the Mayo Clinic way off in Rochester, Minnesota, but they didn't. They took her home, instead.

Marcella slept a lot, and read. When she felt stronger, she began to play with Lucille some, and to do her schoolwork so she wouldn't fall too far behind. Sometimes she tried to get out of bed, but as soon as she stirred, the fever would rise. So she stayed put: eating off a tray, using a bedpan, lying under the sunlamp, just in case it was TB. But mostly she slept. And tried not to think about what had caused it.

She knew, of course, that this was God's punishment, but she dared not tell, even when the doctors asked her all sorts of questions. She was too ashamed. Besides, what could you prescribe for a sin of commission? You could only pray, which she did, and she memorized many Bible verses.

Christmas came and went, and the new year turned, and it snowed some more. Then one day—you could already smell the beginnings of spring in the March air—her mother took her out on the back porch, all bundled with blankets, and let her sit in the swing awhile, facing the sun. She drank it. The sun, the warm almost-spring sun on her face. And as she swung slowly, back and forth, she heard the faint sounds of *I come to the gar – den a – lone,* way in the back of her head. She was amazed. So He *did* love her, at least a little bit, and she knew the sickness was almost over, and that she would be back to school before the month was done.

The fever lifted as miraculously as it had descended. The songs returned; she went back to playing her piano. But the experience left its mark. How could she dismiss weeks, *months,* in bed? God didn't fool around with sin of commission sinners, she could see that.

When she got back to school, things had changed.

Slam books were a big thing; all the seventh graders had them. You wrote somebody's name on a page and passed the book around, and everybody'd write down stuff like "she's cute" or "PU she stinks." Cheryl wrote down "Marcella" and passed her book around. Nobody said much of anything nice. "Sickly Celery," they wrote, and "thinks she's so good," and a couple of boys got it and wrote back and forth:

"What was she doing at home all that time?"

"She wasn't home. She was down in the piney woods with Mr. Drew." (Mr. Drew was the school janitor.)

"Where's the baby?"

"Come on, Marcella, show it to us. We won't tell. Ha, ha."

At least nobody wrote PU. Just the same, she hid those pages from Lucille.

Another thing that had changed were the boys, always passing dirty notes and chasing girls into the cloakroom so they could kiss you, but you better not let them, Karen Harding said in the water line after recess, because you can get pregnant if a boy kisses you. Cheryl said that wasn't true—only if there was an eclipse, or if he tried to tongue you. "Tongue" you? What did that mean? Everybody seemed to know but Marcella. And there were other words, strange ones, like "the curse." All the girls talked about it. She thought maybe it was a disease going around. Maybe that's what she had, the curse, and the doctors hadn't known about it yet, because she was first. And "little eggs" and "come on" smiles, and "bedroom eyes." What did it all mean?

Some she knew. Cheryl told her. "Flashlight" was a boy's thing, so if somebody passed you a note that said, "Can I put my flashlight on your tongue and look for my red wagon?" you were supposed to get up and slap him, even if it was during class. And "whale tail." That's what Ada Rosenstatt had, a big behind. The boys teased her all the time, "Hey, whale tail. Wanta puff of my cigar?" White Owl cigar—that means a boy's you-know-what, too.

Everybody was talking dirty now, not just Cheryl. In line at the water fountain, kids would whisper stuff. The girls, even, told jokes in the bathroom. About Johnny Fuckerfaster, who was doing it to a girl, and his mother caught them, and she said, "Johnny Fuckerfaster!" And he said, "But ma! I'm fucking her as fast as I can!" And about the old witch who lived in a cave and did it with ears of corn, and then ate them. "If you think the corn's bad, you oughtta taste the butter." Marcella didn't get that one. She tried to find out from Cheryl, but Cheryl called her dopey. They walked home together, just the same, hiding from Lucille. Lucille was such a pest, always wanting to tag along, but you couldn't talk about *anything* with a little sister around.

"Know what Tommy Edwards said?" Marcella asked one day.

"Nope," said Cheryl, "and I don't care."

"He said to tell you that Ralph says you've got bedroom eyes."

That got her.

"Boy, just let him say that to my face, I'll give him such a smack! Right where it hurts, too. Want a Life Saver?...No, not that one. Oranges are my favorites."

Marcella found a lemon one halfway down, and popped it in her mouth. "How come old lady Stuyvesant didn't make Linda play volleyball?" she asked, sticking the Life Saver between her teeth and cheek to melt.

"'Cause she's on the rag," said Cheryl, spinning out around a lamppost before they crossed the street.

"On what?"

"On the rag. Off the roof. Menstruating." They crossed the street, up, over the curbstones. They didn't walk on them any more.

"Menstrating?"

"Men – *stru* – ating, dopey. Cripes. Don't tell me you never heard of that, either?"

Marcella shook her head.

"Well, it's when you bleed."

"*Bleed?*" Marcella stopped dead still on the sidewalk. "Linda was *bleeding?* Why didn't anyone…"

"Hey, stupe, what's the matter with you? Haven't you ever heard of bleeding? Or anything?"

Marcella said nothing. They walked on. Cheryl jumped up and tried to touch the branch on the Randall lawn, the one that hung down over the sidewalk, but she still couldn't quite, and said:

"Well, you are too dumb for words. I'm not telling you. It'd probably make you sick again. You'd just throw up or something and your mother'd blame it on me."

"No she wouldn't. I won't tell."

"Why don't you ask Lucille, then. I'll bet she knows."

"Come on, Cheryl, please! Just this once."

"You are so dumb, I don't even know why I walk home with you any more."

"I'll let you copy my arithmetic." They were nearing the corner where Cheryl turned off.

"Old Celery's got the curse; fal – ling off the roo – oof! A Little Egg Ran Up Her Leg and –"

Marcella clapped her hands over her ears.

"Ask your mother, baby."

"My mother?"

Cheryl began to mimic: "My mo – ther? My mom – ma! Idgim widgims gotta ask her mom – ma?" Then Cheryl's voiced suddenly turned strident: "Better ask your mo – ther, dopey. Cripes, *Everybody* knows."

So Marcella asked.

Afterward she wished she hadn't: Mrs. Colby's coffee cup clattering on its saucer, her face turning frosty.

"Where did you hear about that?"

Shifting back and forth, one foot and then the other. She daren't mention Cheryl.

"From the kids at school. They said I better ask you." Explaining. About Linda not playing volleyball. So her mother wouldn't think it was like the slip. Maybe it was like the slip, as bad as fuck, as filthy, and Cheryl'd tricked her into asking. "I didn't tell Lucille."

"I see," said Mrs. Colby, and she sat motionless awhile, staring at the crossword-puzzle book in front of her. Marcella thought she wasn't going to say anything else, and maybe it was time to leave, when Mrs. Colby looked up:

"Well, don't just stand there. It's nothing you have to know about this very minute. When the time comes, I'll explain it to you."

But Marcella figured out some of it anyway. Sort of. "Period." That's what the ninth-grade girls called it, in the restroom, combing their hair and talking to each other, "having my period," or "Oh, no! The curse!" or "those days," as in "one of *those* days again." You could tell what they meant by the way they drew out "those" real long, making it sound like a bother. Sometimes they joked about it. "On the rag again? Brother, I'm glad I'm not." One girl told a story about three society women, sipping tea with little fingers curled, and bragging about who was the daintiest.

"I have such tiny feet," said the first. "Only size three. I can't get shoes small enough to fit me anywhere."

"With me it's my hands," said the second. "My hands are so small I have to have my gloves 'specially made."

The third lady excused herself, and went to the bathroom. When she came back, she said, "Oh, sorry to bother you, but do either of you have a Band-Aid? My period started."

The ninth-grade girls laughed and laughed about that one, but Marcella wasn't too sure what it meant, only the part about bleeding, and she couldn't figure out what the "rag" was, or if there really was one. A lot of seventh-grade girls were already "on it," not just Linda, but, well, practically everybody, even Karen Harding, acting so stuck-up because she knew what it meant. Marcella pretended to know, too. She didn't really lie about it. Lying was too big a sin. She just pretended, and said "yes" when Cheryl asked if she'd asked her mom – ma. She didn't say that Mrs. Colby hadn't told her.

She learned that periods have lots of rules. You don't have to go to school the first time it happens to you, that's one rule. Except Patty. Patty got the curse, and her mother made her go to school the first day, and everybody knew, even though she was too embarrassed to tell, sitting in the restroom, crying, and not coming out for recess, even though everybody told her she had to. But she wouldn't. She was too scared to tell Mrs. Stuyvesant.

When the kids called Mrs. Stuyvesant and told her, Patty locked herself into one of the stalls and wouldn't come out, not even for the teacher. So finally they left her sitting there. She stayed until recess was over, then she came in and sat at her desk, trying not to cry. She didn't raise her hand once for questions in geography class, and the funny thing was Mrs. Stuyvesant. She didn't call on Patty, not at all, and usually, oh boy, just keep your hand down, and old lady Stuyvesant would call you right away.

Not having to play at recess was a regular school rule. You have to tell Mrs. Stuyvesant, and sit on the sidelines where everyone looks at you and knows you have the curse, but if you play, and run and jump around, then blood runs down your legs and the boys see it and everything. That's what Cheryl said, but Marcella saw Linda running home one day after she sat out at recess, and there was no blood, not anywhere.

Cheryl had a joke about it: "Oh, a little egg ran down her leg," meaning *blood*, and she wouldn't say the rest, but the boys, oh, the eighth-grade boys, especially, they said it backwards: 'Oh, that little egg ran *up* her leg, and fucked her once, and fucked her twice, and fucked her oh so very nice," but everybody would squeal, and cover their ears as soon as they heard *up*, instead of *down*, so they couldn't hear the filthy word. They squealed so loud it took Marcella several days to figure out the whole song, through her hands over her ears. Such a bad song that the boys, even the eighth-grade boys, never dared chant it in the schoolyard, for what if one of the teachers heard them? Or Mr. Cooper, the principal? So they only said it on their way home.

That was why the girls had to keep close together. Karen Harding and Linda and that bunch even let Cheryl and Marcella walk real close to them, especially when eighth grade got out early, and especially the second and third block home before the kids started turning off in different directions, because if you didn't stick close together, and the boys found you, they would put something worse than little eggs on you, that's what Cheryl said. She and Marcella even told Lucille that, after school, and at ballgames in the ballpark, you had to remember to watch out, and not go behind the stands by yourself when you wanted to get a Coke or they'd catch you, and do it to you there, too, right under the stands and everything. Even if you didn't *want* to, they'd make you.

Marcella had forgotten all about asking Mrs. Colby when her mother took her into the master bedroom "to talk about a few things." Mrs. Colby sat on the edge of the huge double bed, "Here, Marcella, sit down," and patted the chenille spread, the color of dusty rose. Mrs. Colby's favorite color, rose, like the wallpaper.

Marcella sat down gingerly. Something was wrong, she could feel it, so she said nothing, she just stared at the bedspread. The tufts made swirling patterns, round and round, back and back, toward the headboard. Mrs. Colby ran her finger along the ridge of the chenille, bending the tufts down to the plain part, and lifting them, over and over again. Beginning to speak:

"Women," she said, "are different from men, in lots of different ways. You know that."

"Yes," Marcella said, avoiding her mother's eyes as cautiously as Mrs. Colby avoided Marcella's.

"And one of the things women have to do is have babies. God made them that way. Do you know about having babies?"

What was she asking *that* for. Who didn't know what mothers told you about babies, brought in the night by a big stork? There was even a picture of it in the doctor's office, Mrs. Colby had pointed it out to her, the stork a shadow of the doctor, only Cheryl said from boys kissing you, except you have to eat their seeds under a blanket or it doesn't work, but Linda said you get babies in your *belly*. And it didn't matter whose seeds you ate. Even watermelon seeds...but that didn't seem right.

"Yes."

"Oh." Where could Marcella have picked that up? From hearing all those filthy farm boys talk about their cattle, she supposed. Or maybe from Cheryl. "Then we don't need to discuss that."

The silence seemed to last a long time. Mrs. Colby began once more:

"Well, babies, when God puts them inside you, are fed by your placenta. The placenta is food for the baby. That's why we have navels, you know. The navel is where the umbilical cord is attached. It is clipped after birth, and tied."

Mrs. Colby felt herself veering way off track. She took a long breath, and made herself calm down, but when she tried speaking again, the words came out more rapidly than before.

And the more Mrs. Colby talked, the more uncertain Marcella became. What had she done? Said something she shouldn't, about men and women doing it? About babies? But she'd never mentioned the watermelon seed, not even to Lucille...

"Now that is the way that God made women, so they feed their babies through the placenta, and every twenty-eight days, whether you have a baby or not, I mean after you become a woman, God puts the placenta in your womb, so that if a child is conceived, if you are married, of course, and conceive, then there will be food for it. Now if there is no child, even if you are not married, then the placenta drops out."

Mrs. Colby stopped abruptly. Marcella looked up. Her mother returned the glance. Both were embarrassed: Marcella's face was flushed, and Mrs. Colby began twisting one of the tufts, round and round. Marcella didn't know what she was supposed to say. Finally Mrs. Colby asked, "Do you understand?"

Marcella thought a minute, then decided to be truthful.

"No," she said, looking quickly down again.

"Well, it's really very simple," Mrs. Colby said, half in exasperation, half in frustration, not knowing *how* you were supposed to explain these things, certainly these things had never been explained to *her*, she had nearly fainted from fright when she discovered blood in her pants, fearing a hemorrhage or worse...

"The placenta is the part that comes out when you are menstruating."

Menstruating. Menstruating. The word seemed, for a moment, foreign. Then it took on Cheryl's sing-song tone: men – *stru* – ating. Ask your mom – ma. Cheryl! And Linda! Linda? Placenta comes out? Out of...

"It comes *out?* she asked, her voice pitched high from fright. "Out? Where? Here?" touching herself on a nipple, because that's where babies are fed, and Linda, such big ones, rising high in the air when she leaped for the volleyball, almost as big as Rosemary's, and still in grade school...

"No, no. Of course not there. That's for milk."

"But if it feeds the baby..."

"When it's *inside* you, Marcella, when the baby is growing *inside* you, that's where God puts the placenta, in your *womb*, for the child to be nourished by – through his umbilical cord."

Inside you? And why was her mother so angry...then Linda was right, in the *belly!*... Marcella was sure she hadn't said anything wrong, not about babies, or feeding babies, or breasts at all except...in your BELLY? how does it get OUT? does the doctor OPEN you? Is that what the blood is for? And the rags? And the Band-Aid?... except for that day after school, asking, "What does menstruating mean?" oh, she must have made her mother mad, asking about it, but out? *where?* how...can it come. No. No sense. No sense at all.

"But where does it come out, the menstruating?"

Mrs. Colby stopped twisting the chenille tufts, and sat up very straight. Taking advantage of her, that was all, of her liberality in speaking directly about these things. Should never have. Something *her* mother certainly had never done, perhaps for just such a reason, never explaining things, only "Here. Put this on," leaving her to struggle by herself with...Mrs. Colby's voice became stiff.

"It comes out the vagina, Marcella."

The vagina? The vagina? Bellybutton was navel, but vagina?

"Where is that?" she asked in the smallest voice she owned.

"I thought you knew all about babies." Mrs. Colby did not attempt to conceal her scorn.

"Oh, well, yes I *do*," hastily, not wanting her mother to laugh, like her father always did, like Cheryl, laughing when Marcella said the stork, and didn't even *know*, out of the bellybutton, everybody knows, dopey, first you swallow the seed, and then your stomach gets big as a balloon, and then the doctor comes and there isn't any stork, but the doctor opens up the bellybutton and takes the baby right out —

"I just forgot about vaginas, that's all."

"Well, that's where the babies come out, Marcella." This whole conversation was getting most distressing. "It's no different. Where babies emerge, that's all. Between your legs."

She stood up, and began walking to the door.

"Between your...!!!" Frantically, then, watching Mrs. Colby's back, disappearing. "But what does it look like?"

"Well," Mrs. Colby turned, "it's red...and it looks a little like..." No. Better not say that. "It's just red, that's all. A red discharge."

Better get her a book. A book could explain it more clearly. She should never have begun. Oh, well, everybody makes mistakes with the first child...

She went out, and closed the door.

So it was true, the blood, oh! Out of you, right between your legs, shooting out, like pee! shooting out like water when your thumb's on the end of the garden hose, did it come out of the pee hole? No, the baby hole, her mother said, oh! She was astounded at the idea, and it running down your legs, and how do you stop it, you must have to wait until it comes, until the twenty-eight days are up, that's probably what they are doing at recess, waiting, counting the days like mothers who know when kids are about to be born, and waiting...for it to shoot out, and rags? rags, to mop it up afterward, how much was there? And what if it came right during class? Oh, and maybe stuffing rags in your pants to keep the blood from shooting all over the place, a fountain, and the Band-Aid, of course, for after, when it's all done –

Dear God, oh, dear God in heaven, please, no, don't let it happen to me, the blood, spurting all over like no! I don't want to have babies, so you don't have to bother to put their food in and everything, and then I won't

Hoping, hope against hope, that maybe she wouldn't have to, that maybe God would wait at least until she wanted to have a baby, or maybe pass right over her, like He had passed over those Israelites' houses, marked with blood, oh! Is that what that means?

Praying, on her knees, praying, so afraid that the blood, might, at any time, place, come cascading out of her, what would she do? She felt sick, sick again, yes, running a fever, maybe staying home from school, yes, could, until it happened, but of course not, no, her mother would never let her, but maybe anyway not all girls got it, only some, because she hadn't, and neither had Cheryl, or Donna, or Jeannie, even Ruby hadn't, and Ruby was a whole year older than everybody because she got set back a year, so maybe

Dear God, almighty Father, lover of all your little children here on earth, please let this be a cross I do not have to bear. Please pass over me, like you've passed over Donna, and Cheryl, please make me like Ruby, and not have to at all

It happened very simply, actually. One morning, after she got up, dressed, and went to the bathroom, while she was just sitting there, on the toilet, and reading the label inside the Halo shampoo, her Wednesday underpants dropped down on the linoleum tiled floor between her legs. And after she finished tipping the shampoo bottle back and forth, making the letters on the back of the label turn squiggly through the liquid, she noticed this stain on her pants. At first, she didn't understand what it was, because it didn't look red. Of course, she had on her Wednesday underpants, blue ones because Wednesday's child is full of woe, and that must be why the stain looked more brown than red, but she didn't know what it was. She thought she might have sat on something, but the pants were clean, fresh out of the bureau drawer, so she hadn't had time to sit on anything...She peered down into the toilet bowl.

There it was—a filmy spiral dropping down through water, like egg yolk going into a steaming poaching pan, but red. A spiral of red stuff, hanging there in the water...men – stru – a – tion. The curse! Red as blood. Her mother wouldn't say blood, but the girls at school did.... Well. Here it was, her first period, not shooting out like a garden hose after all, but only dribbling. Now anyway. She was on the rag, whatever that was. Fallen off the roof. Same as Patty. And Linda. And the high-school girls, oh, no, God hadn't passed her by, not even with all the praying.

She started to get up, to go to tell her mother, but stopped halfway. What if it shot out when she began walking? How much stuff came out, anyway? All down your *legs*, Cheryl said. Must be a lot. Oh, her pants would be filthy, and what would her mother say if she soiled them like a baby! Plenty mad. And how do you tell, anyway, that it's coming? Is that what "come" means, your period coming? Not knowing, not knowing what to do, afraid to move, no use hollering, everybody down in the kitchen already but her, they'd never hear her, and there was nothing she could do but sit. And wait.

Downstairs, Mrs. Colby had set the kitchen table for the girls. She was out of Shredded Ralston—Marcella had eaten the last morsel yesterday—so she had put out Rice Krispies (Lucille's favorite) and Corn Flakes. Marcella could choose what suited her. She had set out milk and Ovaltine, and gone to the foot of the stairs and called, "Breakfast," for Marcella's benefit. Lucille was already at the table, waiting for Mrs. Colby to shake up the milk bottle, mix the creamy top milk with the thin milk below. "Where's your sister?"

"In the bathroom. Do I have to wait?"

"No. Go ahead."

Mrs. Colby watched Lucille pour the milk slowly, bending her head down to hear Snap, Crackle, and Pop in her cereal bowl. Lucille turned the box around to the back, and began to read and eat. Mrs. Colby cleaned up: doused the frying pan in hot sudsy water to soak, stacked Mr. Colby's breakfast dishes, rinsed the coffee maker. Such a bother. Why couldn't he drink Nescafé? So fussy. Had to have it brewed, and thick as syrup, too. Thought restaurant coffee was better than her "colored water," that's what he called it. Never mind. He could very well drink her colored water, if he was going to be so picky about Nescafé. She turned around:

"What's keeping Marcella?"

"I don't know," said Lucille, looking up from her cereal box.

"Better go see," said Mrs. Colby.

Marcella had read every word of the labels on the Halo and Drene shampoos, and the Thrushay hand lotion. She had scratched off the "m" in Irium on the Pepsodent tube, the metal underneath so neat, much nicer than the paint, but she put the toothpaste back anyway, so she wouldn't get caught.

She began thinking about how she was wearing her Wednesday pants on Wednesday. She used to do that all the time, after Mrs. Colby gave her the set for Christmas, seven pairs of pants and each a different color—Wednesday's blue, and Thursday's yellow, and Friday's pink, they were nothing special, she had lots of pink pants, all her other pants were pink cotton, but Monday's were lavender, and Sundays! Oh, Sunday's were her favorites, white for purity, and for fair and wise, with red double-hearts embroidered in one corner, with an arrow running through. They all had hearts, and she used to wear Sunday's only on Sunday, and Monday's child is fair of face lavender only on Monday, and Tuesday's only on Tuesday, but she'd gotten out of the habit.

Maybe she'd start again, wearing Thursday's tomorrow, green ones, only she'd have to get a clean pair for Wednesday now...

The bathroom door swung open. Lucille hadn't even knocked!

"Go away!" said Marcella, yanking her skirt down over her knees. "Can't you see I'm going to the bathroom?"

"Mother says what's the matter, did you fall in?"

Marcella tried to stare her down. It didn't work.

"Anyway," Lucille said, "you're supposed to come to breakfast, that's what."

"Well, I can't."

"Well, you have to. That's what mother says."

"Well, I can't."

"Well, you have to, or anyway, you'll be late to school."

Lucille sucked her bottom lip way in and crossed her eyes making a "beeber hawk." Then she thumbed her nose and left.

So eventually Mrs. Colby came up the stairs, angry that she had to climb the flight for "no good reason at all," angry that Marcella refused to budge from the bathroom, even when she was called.

"Well, young lady, and what is the meaning of this?"

"I think I'm..." but Marcella couldn't bring herself to say the word, suppose that she was wrong. "Here. Look. I think something's the matter..." She pointed at her Wednesday pants.

"Oh, goodness!" Mrs. Colby began fluttering around like she always did when the girls were cut, or had stickers, or fell down and scraped the skin off a knee. "Well, sit still, don't move, don't get off, you'll drop on everything, here, you stay there. I'll be right back."

Marcella half-listened to her mother call over the banister: "Lucille? Come here...Lucille, you go on to school. Marcella isn't going to go...She's sick...Just say she's sick, that's all, if her teacher asks. She's sick and she has to stay home...All right. Have a nice day...Yes. Goodbye."

And if a woman have an issue, and her issue in her flesh be blood, she shall be put apart seven days...

Mrs. Colby began talking almost immediately as she came through the door. "Well, here, now, I guess you can use this one of mine. It's clean. Just washed. And later today I'll go downtown and buy you a new one."

"What's that?" Marcella looked in dismay at the tangle of pink elastic, all bands and safety pins, curling over itself. It looked like her garter belt, only ugly.

"It's a Kotex belt. You wear it to keep the napkin on. Here. Give me your panties. Well, I certainly didn't think this would happen so soon. And step right into...here. Stand up. That'll be all right. Oh, you can hold some toilet paper over yourself if you think you're going to drip. There. Now step in." Mrs. Colby pulled the belt up to Marcella's waist, and flattened it, so the elastic wasn't all twisted around. She showed her daughter the difference between the front and the back, the front piece longer, the back one shorter and thicker, and how to pull the metal to adjust the middle band.

And whosoever toucheth her shall be unclean until the even...

"Now here's where I keep the Kotex." Mrs. Colby reached behind the toilet and pulled out the blue-and-white box that had been there as long as Marcella could remember. Blue, and white, like hospitals, like boxes of cotton balls and Q-tips—all that sanitary stuff was blue and white. She had always thought the big gauzes inside were for bandages, in case anyone should ever cut his toe off, or his thumb, like Mr. Colby pretended he'd done once, but it was only a joke, even if her mother had covered her eyes and shrieked, but that's not what these gauzes were for. They were for...

Marcella withered. The gauzes looked like the most gigantic bandages she'd ever seen. Like maybe if you cut off an *arm*. Boy oh boy, you must bleed a terrific amount…these weren't Band-Aids, they were more like diapers.

The gauze made a funny sound, being pulled away from its mates in the package.

"Here. This goes outside." Mrs. Colby showed Marcella how the gauze was wrapped around the pad so the loose edges were on one side. "If you put them next to your body, the edges might open, and all that…discharge would go directly on the pad."

"Isn't there a rag?" Marcella asked.

"A rag? Whatever gave you that idea? No, nobody has used rags since the First World War. Oh, your grandmother did, but I didn't have to. Here."

Mrs. Colby showed Marcella how to fold the ends before she pinned them—the front ends only a little bit, enough to hold the safety pin, but not too much. That pulls the pad up to your belly, which is no fun at all. Then the back part, which is more difficult to get right, and more important, because if you don't get it right, the pin will come open and stick you, and that is most uncomfortable, so pay attention to what I'm saying and don't wiggle around so much, you have to fold the back part *way down,* but not all the way, because if you fold it too much, it will be too thick and you can't get the safety pin through it, but you have to—

"Do stand still, Marcella! This wiggling around doesn't help."

But she couldn't stand still. It felt like a pillow, like an enormous pillow being stuffed between her legs, how could she begin to walk with it on, she'd have to walk bowlegged and everybody would *know* what she was wearing, how could the girls *stand* it —

"Now pay attention. You have to pull the elastic way down in back—here, watch what I'm doing—and stick the pin in this way. See? With the point *up*. That way, if the pin opens, it won't be so likely to stick you."

"But if the pin opens"—oh, what if!—"everything will fall right out! Anybody could see it!"

"Nonsense. Your pants will hold it up, at least long enough to get to the bathroom and fix it."

"Oh." So you wore pants, too. "But Mrs. Stuyvesant won't let us go to the bathroom, she doesn't let anybody go except at recess."

"Don't be silly. Just tell her what the problem is, and she'll let you."

But Marcella couldn't imagine what she would say to her teacher, how awful, going to school with this thing on, trying to walk with it between your legs, not able to play or anything. Not even swing on the bars. Patty, in the bathroom, crying.

And every thing that she lieth upon in her separation shall be unclean: every thing also that she sitteth upon shall be unclean...

"There," said Mrs. Colby, patting the last piece of elastic in place. "We're finished."

Marcella stood, afraid to move. The Kotex was jammed between her legs, the tension on the elastic pulled the belt down so it rode in huge Y's, on her stomach, and behind, with the back strap so tight it pulled the gauze way up high between her cheeks.

"Now pull your underpants up," said her mother.

"I can't!" Marcella wailed. "I can't even bend over!"

"Nonsense," said her mother, but she pulled them up for Marcella anyway, feeling pity for the transition that her daughter was making into that sorry state of womanhood she'd have to bear, month after month, coming in to discover that it was time, again, to don the old harness. Still and all, it was better than her mother had known, with no Kotex at all, using cloths instead, the cloths so precious they had to be washed, whew! She could still remember the odor of the soiled material hitting the boiling water, and never, no matter what, able to remove the stains, and so ashamed when she finally understood what they were, what her mother had been hanging on the clothesline all those years as though they were merely handkerchiefs. She'd never gotten over her embarrassment about that. At least Marcella…

"Now go change into a full skirt."

"Can't I wear my jeans? I don't have to go to school."

"No. You can see the belt right through the jeans. And through tight skirts. You don't want everybody to know, do you?" Marcella shook her head. "So run along, now, and find a nice full skirt to wear, so the elastic won't show through."

Marcella stayed home all day. She found out she couldn't go outdoors and play, because too much running around makes you bleed too hard. And you can't climb trees or ride bikes, anyway, in a full skirt. But it wasn't as hard to walk as she'd feared: the Kotex bent in two, lengthwise, making a ridge that cut into her crotch a little, but it also made the pad narrower, so she could even sit down and cross her legs, and everything.

"I can't play dolls with you," she told Lucille when she had come home from school for lunch.

"Why not?"

"Because…I can't tell. You're too young. It's something only *women* know."

Lucille left in a huff.

When Marcella had to go to the bathroom, Mrs. Colby came with her and showed her how to fold the napkin in half so you wouldn't mess yourself, and then just sit and hold it out front while you went, and then put it back on again. That part made Marcella a little sick to her stomach, because the blood wasn't red like she thought it would be, but brown, and slick. Her mother made her put the pad back on anyway. You change them twice a day, Mrs. Colby said, and that's enough. Except maybe, later, when you get older, if you flow harder, you might have to use three or even four on the first day, and sometimes on the second, but now, you don't have to worry because you are just beginning. Mrs. Colby explained how to fold the pad and wrap it with toilet paper when you discard it, and how menstruation happens every twenty-eight days, only maybe at first it won't be so regular. And how Marcella couldn't stay home from school *every* time it happened.

And whosoever toucheth her bed shall wash his clothes, and bathe himself in water, and be unclean until the even.

It wasn't much fun after lunch, staying home, because she couldn't run around or anything. Mostly she practiced her piano lessons a bit, and memorized some Bible verses, and read some. When Mrs. Colby went out, she played dolls. Her mother never let her. She was getting too old for such things, Mrs. Colby said, although she still let her play dolls with Lucille, to keep Lucille quiet.

When Mrs. Colby got back, Marcella was waiting.

"Please don't tell Daddy about this, will you?" she said, flushing. "Please."

Mrs. Colby eyed her sharply. "We'll see," was all she would reply. Marcella could hardly eat her supper that night for fear she told, and that he knew...for fear he was looking right into her...

She stayed home the second day, too, because the flow suddenly—and quite surprisingly, for the first time, her mother said—became heavy, and with it came such aches. Her whole body ached. It was like having the flu, without any fever. She would get used to it, Mrs. Colby said, but Marcella didn't think so, staying in bed nearly all day.

To pass the time, she read the "continued" story in the *Ladies Home Journal,* but the last installment hadn't come yet, so she didn't know how it ended. She pored over the sanitary-napkins ads—she'd never read them before—and passed Kotex's "Are You in the Know?" test successfully, which made her feel good. She thought about sending away for the Modess booklet, "Growing Up and Liking It!" but she didn't. She saw some other ads, for stuff you could use and even go swimming (at "those" times), so she figured out that you couldn't swim with a Kotex on. But that was okay. There was no place to swim, anyway, except the river when it ran high enough, but Mrs. Colby never let her. Water too dirty.

Marcella tried to comfort herself by reading the *Saturday Evening Post* cartoons, but she was not comforted. It was so awful, menstruating. And unclean. Even the Bible said so, unclean, along with the cloven-footed and the swine, the mouse and the ferret, along with scales, and plague, and especially leprosy. Ugh. And nothing she could do about it. Nothing. It was like knowing you were going to be sick, month after month after month, and not being able to play, and having people make fun of you...she couldn't believe how bad it was. Mrs. Colby told her she should get out of bed, she couldn't possibly be having cramps, she was too young for that, that came when you got older. But Marcella stayed in bed, curled up into a ball and hugging herself, feeling better in that position than in any other way.

And whosoever toucheth any thing that she sat upon shall wash his clothes, and bathe himself in water, and be unclean until the even...

When Friday came, she was bleeding hardly at all. What a relief! But Mrs. Colby said she'd better wear the Kotex anyway, just in case. She said Marcella had to go to school, too, but Marcella protested so vehemently that Mrs. Colby gave in. After all, she thought, it was Marcella's first time, and there was a lot to absorb. Still, "don't think you get to stay home every time," she said, "because you don't. Having your period is nothing to stay home for. You simply go about your business as usual, and pretend that nothing is happening."

Actually, Marcella didn't really want to stay home another day, but the thought of going back to school still strapped in that diaper, and having to face all her classmates, and sit out at recess, and everybody able to tell, anyway, because of the full skirt she had to wear, and them *knowing* she hadn't been sick...it was too much to face. But staying home was really boring, especially with Lucille away. She even wished she had some homework to do.

She flipped through *Good Housekeeping,* and read all the jokes at the bottom of the pages in *Reader's Digest,* and then she still didn't know what to do, so she went upstairs and sat at her dresser, staring in the mirror and practicing winking. She didn't think she'd ever get it. Whistling had been easier to learn. She decided to pluck her eyebrows, like the ladies in the magazines. She got the tweezers and Mrs. Colby's magnifying mirror, and pulled out nearly a half-dozen hairs. That really hurt! The effort turned her skin lobster red. So she stopped, and finally asked her mother to bring her some books from the library. *The Farm Twins,* she wanted, by Lucy Fitch Perkins, her favorite-in-the-whole-world book, she never tired of reading it, but her mother said no, that was for Lucille's age, Marcella was old enough to read more serious books. Mrs. Colby brought home *Little Women,* instead. It was okay, except the girls were all so good, she got a little tired of them...

And on the eighth day, she shall take unto her two turtles, or two young pigeons, and bring them unto the priest, to the door of the tabernacle...And the priest shall offer the one for a sin offering, and the other for a burnt offering...

Saturday morning was one of the happiest days of her life. She had no period at all Friday afternoon, so her Kotex was still white when she went to bed, but Mrs. Colby said she'd better wear it anyway, because there was no sense getting the sheets all messy. Then, Saturday morning, the napkin was *still* white! but Mrs. Colby said, better wait and see after breakfast, because sometimes it is like that in the morning and you think you're finished, but then you're not. So wait and see.

Marcella waited until she'd eaten her cereal and toast, then ran upstairs. Still white! She was done! Wednesday, Thursday, Friday, Saturday—her mother had told her she probably wouldn't be through until Sunday, it usually ends on the fifth day, but here it was, only Saturday, only Saturday morning, and she was finished, all done, through, and could go outside and climb trees and play and everything.

Mrs. Colby said there was no need to save the white pad, so Marcella folded it, like the others, and wrapped it up, too, so it wouldn't fall open. That way nobody in the bathroom could happen to see it. Then she climbed into her jeans, oh, how good they felt, and ran outdoors in the sunshine to play. First she rode her bike all around the block, twice, fast. After that she thought about roller-skating, but decided to wait until afternoon, and then she climbed up the big elm into her tree house—not really a house, but only a platform. It had been there as long as she could remember.

She lay flat on her stomach, and looked down...watching old Mr. Lucharm walk by, probably on his way to the post office to check his mail, down and back every day at the same time: late morning, but not too late, but not so early that the mail wouldn't be sorted yet...watching her mother come out and pin a few clothes to the line, her mother not seeing her, Marcella giggling, but holding it back...watching old Mrs. Schneider next door out hoeing the garden, scratching around in the dirt, though Mr. Colby said what with all her chickens scratching around, he didn't understand why she had to, too...remembering, the way that old lady would slaughter her chickens, how she would grab one, when it least expected, grab one right around its head, hands covering its beady eyes, beak, crest, everything, twisting its neck like a big cable, then down, down on the ground, swift as lightning her black shoe on its head, smash, worn sole of the high-topped shoe, small, old shoes, sometimes laced with brown laces, smash, the chicken's cheek into the ground and chop! one stroke, only, and blood shooting through the air, and down, big blobs of blood hitting the ground and gathering the dust to them, like the first big drops of summer rain make little pools of mud, only this blood-mud, and the chicken, oh! Still alive! So hard to believe, the headless chickens scampering around the yard like maniacs, and the blood slowing down, until there were just spattered snow-white chickens with red *holes* where heads had been, still running, red gaping holes, and all spattered, their white feathers all spattered with drops of blood...finally, toppling, their bodies still warm.

Lying on her back, looking up, up, through the lacy layers of spring leaves, the light making them almost translucent, but green, still green, that thin spring green of grass when it first sprouts, before the droughts get to it, and the branches, dark, all below the leaves, not hidden like when you draw a tree in school, the branches first, and then the leaves on top...until she tired of that, too. Maybe she would roller-skate after all.

She was walking across the backyard toward the house when she felt it. There. She felt it. It was like...the same thing that happens to your stomach when you go over a steep hill...a dropping. A dropping down, inside of her. Inside. Only not in the stomach. Down. Down, lower. She was almost *certain*...began to run, slamming through the back screen, across the wooden porch, the linoleum, through the dining room, across the living room carpet, the stairs, two at a time, like she was never supposed to do, because she might fall, the varnished steps, but clutching, clutching at the banister so if she did, and finally, at the top, across the wooden hallway, through the bathroom door, onto the toilet...

But she knew, she really knew, after all, and didn't even have to look to know, so she sat down, even before she spread wide to see. There it was. Blood, all red and still wet, in a big stain the shape of an almond, oh a very *large* almond, lying right in the center of the white, oh, so pure white, of her very favorite pair of panties, the Sunday ones that she'd put on today to celebrate, the white ones with red hearts embroidered, Sunday's child is good and gay, with the two hearts, and the arrow going straight through them...again.

Again!

AGAIN!

But her mother had promised her it would be twenty-eight days before...twenty-eight days...before she began, again. Promised. So, maybe, then, it meant, maybe, that she wasn't really *through,* that she wasn't finished yet, that she wouldn't be done until Sunday, five whole days, just like her mother said, with the full skirt, and the tight elastic, and the pin coming undone no matter how carefully she fixed it, it had already stuck her once, right on the tail bone, and that pillow between her legs, and sitting out at recess, and everyone could *tell*...every twenty-eight days, for five days, for the rest of her whole life...yes, that was the way it would be, until she was old, old, as old as grandma had been, as old as Mrs. Schneider, all shriveled up and gray and almost dead...

part
two

❧ 10 ❧

It was her hair that started it, her hair, down there, not sprouting in rows like wheat, but coming in on a slant. And Marcella, struggling to sleep…the hot summer night, the waiting, the porch swing creaking below, and her hair, straight and flat. A lot now, more all the time, making a yellow-brown patch on her body. But she could still see pink underneath, could still almost see how the mound used to look, bare, egg-shaped, smooth as a baby's cheek, just like she could still almost see her no-breasts…her child body nestling right beneath her new one, like an abandoned doll, its shape barely visible under fallen snow. Oh, the smooth pink of her mound skin! How she liked to stroke it, such strange skin, tender as the inside of her elbow, tender as her finger webs, always tingling. The lighter she touched it, the more it tingled, the two mounds underneath her hair, mounds split by that dark line, that crevice, that path running to…nowhere.

All summer long she climbed upstairs and tried to sleep, sticking her hot legs down under the cool white sheets, such incredibly cool sheets on summer nights, cool as high notes on the piano, as…cucumber salad, as refrigerated air, cool as the metal of the ice-water jug, yes, cool as water, trickling, down her throat, trickling and turning into, into, brooks, oh, cool as the icy little brooklets in English storybooks, brooklets she'd never seen, bubbling over her feet, and through the meadow, through the cool green meadow, the water rippling into streams, gurgling and churning, spinning, heaving and tossing, swinging and rocking, rocking, rocking, her bed creaking like the swing, rocking the boat of her body, cool, cool, and serene the sheets, lapping her down the stream and sometimes even into the ocean, the faraway ocean existing only in dreams, or pictures, the ocean, rocking her hot and tumbled body between the cool cool sheets of its waves before she

smoothed down her hair, into flat strands, under her fingers, flat like a stroked eyebrow, pressed hair sticking under her fingertips, then rebounding, tickling so delicately as her fingertips released them, prickling something fierce as one by one, the hairs, sprang back.

Stroking, and stroking, feeling the hair flat against her skin under her nightie, feeling, so good, if only she knew whether God had really forgiven her. If He'd really forgiven her, wouldn't He have passed her by? And she wouldn't have to, every twenty-eight days, like Donna, who still didn't, or Cheryl. Maybe she should ask for forgiveness at communion (oh, she'd taken it maybe six times now, once a month, that's plenty, not every Sunday like Catholics do), maybe she would ask then, for the special forgiveness only communion brings, because the minister asked it for everybody, they call it intercession

sliding in between the cool sheets, waiting until her body warmed them, watching flickering shadows of cottonwood and elm branches on her papered wall, then spreading her legs open in a big Y, the untouched sheets striking like cool water. Waiting. Stroking the hairs flat, tickling, stroking sometimes the mounds on either side of that crack place letting herself drift to sleep. Or, sometimes lifting her nightie way up, letting all that skin—leg skin, body skin, breast skin—touch, then lifting those sheets, high, letting go, letting them drift down, and down, breezing her whole body. Or, tickling. Tickling everywhere, drinking in the cooling sensation her fingers made tracing an arm, a breast, a rib, or, her belly, yes! And down, down, but ever so slowly, prolonging each stroke, like sucking on a caramel, my, what funny little prickles her fingers made, the tingling not just outside, no but rushing up from inside, from deep inside scampering to the surface to kiss her glittering fingertips, oh!

There were so many blessings to thank God for: these summer nights, their quiets broken only by the tree-frog croaks, the rustle of leaves, the drift of voices. Breezes, sometimes from the tiny fan droning across the room, sometimes from the sheets, rising, falling—*Praise God, from whom all bless – ings flow: Praise Him, all creatures here be – low; Praise Him a – bove ye heav – enly host: Praise Fa – ther, Son and Ho – ly Ghost.*

The path.

The path running to nowhere, she could not begin to see where it ended, not even when she sat up and bent way over, such a dark crack, obscured by hair sprouting along either side like wild weed flowers lining the roadway, her fingers blindly following the hair down, and down, and down. When they reached the bottom of that mound, down, she would let one (just one) slip off the shoulder of the road, and she would draw that single finger slowly, back, along the dark path, oh. Only moistness, only softness, soft and moist as the cave of the cheek is to the edge of the tongue, yes. She began sliding her finger down that path, down and up, down and up, but waiting always until *after* she flattened her hair, that's how she began: first flattening, then tiptoeing her fingers and down and down and down, and they arrived, *then* letting one, slip, into the path and

So private. No question of that, more private than powdering after a bath. No one watched her powder, either, not even Lucille, they hadn't seen each other naked since they moved into separate rooms, so long ago. You may *not* go in if the door is closed. Only Mrs. Colby had since then, coming into the bathroom to help Marcella scrub her back, dipping handfuls of water up, the water rushing in rivers down her skin…but no more. So no one knew how she planned it, dipping the bath puff into its round box, gently, so only a few tufts of cloth caught the white grains, then poofing it—biff, biff, biff—white circles on her body, like holy wafers, larger, but every bit as paper-thin as the ones Reverend Chettenforth drops on your tongue, and then slowly, with the palms of her hands, rubbing the powder-wafer round and round and round.

Was it the Holy Ghost she felt at night, wafting in on the breezes? Was it He? His breath, winging his way down her body? but that was probably not true, either, because Reverend Chettenforth said you can't actually see the Holy Ghost, or even feel Him, except in your heart. But the tingling always rose, from lower. Otherwise, it felt a lot like singing Alleluia on Easter morning, so maybe He lives inside each and every one of us, and rises up in different ways…

Her body, against the sheets and her fingers, drifting along her body, along her belly skin, almost as tickly as her inner arms, and then her hair, first the triangle patch, and then the hair sprouting by the edge of the dark moist path, and then

Oh, sometimes she would make herself wait *so long* (but never sleeping) before she

Let one finger

It wasn't as if she *stuck* it there, but only *let* it, let it, drift, down, way, far, back, in between the creases of the mound, and then, very, slowly, yes, ever so slowly at first—at first she let it happen only one time before she went to sleep, that was her way—ever so slowly pulling her finger back up toward her belly, like you might pull a piece of licorice through your lips, gripping tight all around it, but her finger

slipping right on *through,* no matter how tightly she tried to hold it...and then to sleep.

When the new wore off a little, she would sometimes let her finger lie motionless, caught between the two moist-as-a-mouth lips, and she would sort of rock that finger up and down, and hum. The humming was an important part of this, she would think about the song, she would listen to it, and think, and rock her finger, and sometimes she hummed herself to sleep this way, waking when her arm got stiff, finding her finger still carefully lying between...and this was delicious, yes.

Then one night, when she was pulling her finger way up the patch toward her belly, her finger dropped deeper than usual, and caught itself, on a sort of ledge inside her, so it couldn't continue up the path. Oh. She waited a bit. When nothing happened, she wiggled her finger some, and discovered...it was like a secret cavern there, or a tunnel, dropping back and back and back...if she let her finger go on, could she feel the end of the tunnel? But afraid to try, lying there instead, wondering, her finger ever so still, her face flushing. It must be the vagina place. That's what she thought. It must be that vagina place, where the babies come out, and the monthly blood, but she had no idea... how immeasurably soft.

She lay like that, not taking her finger out, not letting it go in, she lay there humming for ever so long before she...let it...slide, slide, down and down and down and down, only it didn't feel down, just at first, then it felt in and in and in and in, deeper and deeper. It was as strange as if she'd awakened to find herself twins.

The more *in* she went, the more immense the softness was, and the more the softness fell away. Until it didn't feel *in* any more, but only around, and there, and still her finger went...on and on and on. It frightened her. She didn't quite know why, frightening, to be so far into...it was still her *self,* so far into herself...She pulled her finger out, but not quite clearly out, and hummed, and dropped it, well, yes, back, *in,* and that felt so lovely she did it once more, out, and *in,* and out, and *in,* ever so gently, humming quite a bit, and slowly...it was as though she were hugging herself. As though her body were hugging her finger, and her finger were hugging her, how strange. She didn't know why it should feel like hugging, but it did...so comforting, more even than when she was small and curled up in her grandma's lap, all enclosed by arms and feeling those gnarled fingers stroking and stroking her forehead, much nicer, so delicious that she did not want ever to stop, stroking in, and out, and in again, over and over, her mind singing her body's song, over and over again, before finally, able, to calm herself enough, to drift, to sleep.

Marcella never mentioned her discovery to anyone. She thought about telling Cheryl once, but she didn't. She was afraid that Cheryl might make a little egg joke about it, or tell Rosemary. Then she began to wonder if "down there" was where the boys weren't supposed to touch you, but that thought was too fantastic, no one would dare touch you *there,* and besides, her mother only said, "You mustn't let them touch you," and that meant you mustn't let them take their pants off and put their things on you, like on your arm, because you aren't even supposed to look at what the dog has, long and skinny and pink sliding right out of its furry case sometimes, and the dog even licking it, but you aren't supposed to notice, but that's what you have to watch out for, those long pink things.

Just the same, she didn't mention anything to Cheryl.

When the new wore off again, Marcella decided to see how deep she could go into the soft hole, into the soft place where the walls are like warm kisses. She found that it was ever so deep. If she lay on her back, she couldn't even reach the bottom. But there were other things to finger, there was a little…she didn't know what to call it, only it was harder than the rest, with surfaces, and when she pushed it flat against her bone, my, how it made her jump! And once, well, when she was thinking how big is it, how deep, I don't even know how deep, then she thought how wide? So instead of putting one finger, she put two. Two slipped in pretty easily, almost as easily as one, and two went a little deeper, as well. Three was the most she could get in, and sometimes, she couldn't even get three in, because there wasn't room, but then she found if she just put two in, and let two drop up and down, in and out, the way they wanted, then pretty soon there was room for three after all.

Still she couldn't find the bottom.

She thought maybe it was a shaft that had no end, maybe it ran clear up into her throat, way up into her mouth, even, but that didn't make sense, because it ought to end, if it was the vagina, it ought to end in the baby place. So she decided to try and see how much deeper, on her stomach, and she turned over, and put her fingers inside, and yes! She could go deeper that way, not clear to the end, but deeper, and her fingers started to speed up, going faster and faster, until they were nearly whipping back and forth.

Then something else took over, and grabbed her, tight, tight, all around her chest, as if someone had slipped up behind her and grabbed her in a hug, but too tightly. So she went back to tickling in the old way, on her back, where there were only tingles and tingles and tingles, and down and down and down, finally into a velvety sleep.

But she had to know, did it end or not: So one night, oh, a week later, she turned onto her stomach, already breathing rapidly from thinking about what might happen if she did it fast, and... This was the experiment: not lying on her stomach, but getting up onto her hands and knees, and reaching. But she couldn't stretch far enough that way, so she dropped her head and shoulders flat down on the bed, but left her haunches high, riding way up into the air, so she could stretch her fingers up and up and up until...yes! It did stop! There was another funny place there, a sort of hard place, a round place, like the one under the ledge, but different, bigger, and when she tickled it, with her finger...but her fear rose up, so she stopped. From the fright. She didn't really know what she feared, except everything was so new, and did everybody have this, this place up inside to go visiting, and to stroke, did everybody have it and just not talk about it, or was it only her with the path that she stroked, and the wet walls that kissed her in return, and the...oh, the tiny baby place that wobbled back and forth and back and forth and made the whole wall kissing place go rippling up and down in funny kind of waves.

She could make the walls ripple, yes, she found out, soon, for each night she could hardly wait to go to bed, hardly wait, for she would do it, yes, she'd do it, every night, all of it, before she went to sleep: first the cool sheets, then the legs in a Y, and the nightie up, and the fingers trickling down, down, down, the belly, tickling, the hair getting curlier and thicker, and down the triangle patch, along the path, humming. She would never think about what she was doing, but only let it happen, she would listen to her melodies, so that everything seemed to occur of its own accord, without her really doing anything, but allowing it: letting her fingers drop into the path, letting them rock and rock and rock there, and humming maybe *Praise God from whom all.* She had to wait (this was one of her rules, she made up lots of rules, now), she had to wait until the whole song was finished, and maybe even a little longer, making the delicious tinglings ripple up and down her body, oh, so slowly, before

she'd let her finger get caught on the ledge, so, like the first time, humming, and in, and slowly out, and in, and slowly out, and then two fingers, and slowly out, and two again, and so, until she was ready for three. But never ready for three on her back, first turning ooooooover, not losing the beat—in, and two, and out, and ooooooover, *three* in, and up on her knees, and *three* up, up high, like her haunches were high, but not right away, no, touching, but not right away, keeping it there instead, feeling how everything got higher, and thinner, and different somehow. She held her breath sometimes, that's how she discovered she could make those walls shudder all by herself—they were part of her, they *were* her, and she could move them, just as she could move her fingers over the piano, up and down inside herself, the hugging feeling giving way to another feeling, like kissing, like real kissing maybe feels…but she was afraid of it, a little scared, still…so she always broke off, suddenly and panting, and rolled back over, and let her fingers softly, slowly, tickle her to sleep.

Gradually, her actions changed, from a wavering, to a…firmer, yes, to a swifter, more passionate moving, of her fingers, on the ledges, and in the baby place, making the ripples leap up, and up, and up again, and she liked them best there, caught right at the crest while she was holding her breath, cramming her head hard down into her pillow, pressing her neck sometimes tight up against the headboard, and then one night—she couldn't believe she had done it—with breath so tight, and stomach pulled in, hard, hard, because the ripples felt so good that way, and with her fingers, oh! letting her fingers go the way they wanted, faster, and faster, that's what they did, racing, racing, in out, in out, in out so swiftly she couldn't even hum, and on and on, the walls hugging so tightly around her three fingers, oh! hugging incredibly tightly, and then, just as she started thinking "time to stop now," then…it began!

It began *doing* it, all alone, it was doing it, she wasn't making the walls ripple ker – *plash*, ker – *plash* against her fingers, no, it was the walls all by themselves! splat, splat, splat, ever so rapidly, faster than she could count, and then it was, oh, those shudders, coming, not like tickling, not like tingling little raindrops glittering through her body, no, oh no, not even like the great warm tidal waves she herself could make against her own fingers, letting them ride out and down the edges of her arms, making her shiver, no, *better* than those, bigger and harder and…oh, enormous wind-torn gusts of feeling that…rumbling! these shudders were nothing like the others. There was no stopping these…coming upon her like the crashing of a hurricane, like the clapping of thunders, like the crescendo of a great herd of buffalo tramping, like…oh! like Mrs. Robinson's organ, when she plays it full blast, and even the floorboards, underfoot, tremble.

No part of her felt the same, after.

She released her breath in such a burst she thought for sure her mother, downstairs, would hear her. She let her exhausted body drop, down against the oh so warm now sheets, her body drenched with perspiration, the room suddenly so cold, and her poor exhausted body that had hunched so hard against the headboard in those last, oh! moments, so hard that a bit of the varnish stuck on the nape of her sweating neck, and she inhaled that tart varnish smell as she rolled over, onto her pillows. Still heaving. Heaving, and panting, and nearly crying with the force of it all...the feelings, all tangled, she began hugging herself, hugging and caressing as though she were her own baby cuddled there, holding herself and stroking and nearly weeping from the strength of the feelings.

When she calmed down enough to hear her own voices, to hear the melody of herself that always sang inside her, the melody didn't sound like a voice, any more, but like an organ, roaring even louder than Mrs. Robinson's: *O God, our help in a – ges past, Our hope for years to come...* so overwhelmingly, filling her whole being even unto the edges of her arms, just as the shudders had done, as strongly, as fully, as clearly, as passionately... *Our shel – ter from the storm – y blast, And our e – ter – nal home...* ebbing, the music, like the feelings had, so hard to tell which was which, until she heard the voices singing again, and felt her own arms still holding herself closely, and this way she rocked herself to sleep.

The next day she thought someone would surely notice, that what she had done would show on her face, but no one said anything, not even Lucille. For days after, thinking about it (she dared not let her fingers explore again, not right away) the experience continued to amaze her. She had no idea what it was, such incredible sensations, from tingling to tickling, from a swelling into a bursting, into such an explosion of feeling that she was swept beyond herself and back, way back, deep into herself. She thought about it, and she prayed about it, thanking God, for she had loved it, and in her memory it became as romantic as a movie love scene, as though she—or something—was even maybe like *kissing* her, but such an ecstatic kiss.

She thought sometimes that what she'd done was wrong, that she shouldn't do it again, that maybe it was like sinning. But how could it be? It was different, so different, this feeling, from her sinning in the church, oh, what a dropping of the tornado of ice on her *that* had been, and not able to think of anything else, how awful, but this was different. How could it be wrong? All bliss, and calm, like floating out on soft warm waters afterward, with heavenly music chorusing in her ears. God must surely approve.

So she let herself. She let her fingers. "Thy will be done, on earth, as it is in heaven." At first, she didn't allow it very often, only every two or three nights, but gradually, as the new wore off, she let herself...oh, every night, after she'd said her prayers.

❧ 11 ❧

Eighth grade turned out to be pretty awful. At first Marcella thought it would be nice, they had a good teacher, Mr. Ipson, who really talked to them, and answered everybody's questions, even "is it true that men come from monkeys," without getting embarrassed, and she got a boyfriend, just like Karen Harding and the other girls. That really felt good, even if he was shorter than her, and only a farm boy. She wrote out her name in round letters—Mrs. Bobby Coleman—like she would if they were married. She let Bobby walk her home from school sometimes, and from Methodist Youth Fellowship nearly every Sunday. Once he took her to a Saturday matinee, but her father didn't like him. Mr. Colby waited inside the door every time Bobby walked her home after dark, he waited until they were about to, maybe to kiss, and then he switched on the front porch light. She never got a goodnight kiss, not one! She didn't know what to do. She got so mad at her father, but she was scared to stand up to him. Finally she broke off with Bobby, instead. "I hate him, I hate him, I hate him," she wrote, about her father, in her diary.

She hoped the rest of the year wouldn't be so bad. She prayed to God to send her a new boyfriend, one that her father would like, or at least to save Cheryl so they could be real friends again, but nothing worked out. Cheryl kept snubbing her more and more, some days nice, and other days not so nice, and nobody else would run around with her, not even the younger kids. Not even Lucille—her own sister!—running with a bunch of sixth grade girls, going everywhere with them, and they wouldn't speak to Marcella, except to tease her and call her "Miss Goody-Good." They were just jealous! She and Lucille began fighting all the time, even though she prayed to God to help her curb her temper. Finally she talked to her mother, but Mrs. Colby said never mind Lucille, it's good for her to have her own friends. So there was nothing much to do after school but study the Bible, and pray, and practice the piano. She practiced so hard on the hymns that Mrs. Colby finally said she could take organ lessons from Mrs. Robinson, if she wanted to. The lessons were about the only good thing that happened that year, the lessons, and what she did every night after prayers.

In the fall, she was in ninth grade now, things got—she couldn't believe it, but it was true—even worse. It started one Saturday when Marcella was still lazing around her room. Someone knocked, it was Mrs. Colby, and she dropped a book on the bed beside Marcella. "Here," she said, "you should find this edifying. Don't let Lucille see it."

At first Marcella couldn't figure out why not, the book looked like a joke book, its pink cover decorated with smiling faces, and old-fashioned curlicued letters. But when she saw the title—*So You're Growing Up*—she knew it was about sex. It had to be. She picked it up gingerly.

Oh, it was like picking up a piece of Mrs. Colby, all gift-wrapped in pink. And under the wrapping, what? Whatever her mother wanted her to know, she supposed. Whatever her mother thought she should have said in all those conversations they never had—they hadn't talked once about sex, not once, since that awful day her mother explained menstruation to her, that terrible day, Marcella perching on the edge of the bed, struggling to understand. She'd been afraid of more talks ever since, afraid of talks about babies, all the girls got that one, or talks about whatever it is that you aren't supposed to let boys do to you, Marcella had been dreading that one ever since she let Bobby walk her home. But the talks never came.

This, instead.

The book was thin, with lots of chapters, and slangy titles, and cartoons decorating the pages—fat bouncing babies, and couples looking like they'd come jitterbugging off the pages of an Archie comic book. Marcella began to read. The first chapter, "Getting to Know You," was all about understanding the very real changes in your body now that you're a teenager. Breasts, for girls, and periods. Voice changes for boys, and something called nocturnal emissions. She'd never heard of them before; the book didn't say what they were.

The next chapter, "From a Little Acorn," looked like it might be better. It was all about babies. Girls have all these eggs inside them, the book said, one for every baby you could make. In clusters? Maybe like those fish eggs her father plucked out of the mother catfish, all clinging together, like amber-brown beads. But it couldn't be true for chickens; they'd get too fat. And each month—after you get to be a teenager—one egg gets ripe and becomes an ovum and comes down, dropped from where the baby eggs are stored inside you, and the ovum sort of floats past this place with hairs waving to keep it on track—the book was pretty vague—and over what looks like a kind of crevice, and through a tunnel, and…but then the author started talking about spermatozoa, ever so tiny, 500 end-to-end make an inch, and skinny. You can put millions of them in a teaspoon. A drawing showed how the spermatozoa penetrates the ovum, and how the ovum attaches itself to the uterus, which is shaped like a pear, and how the cells divide to make a baby. How if two spermatozoa get in by mistake, there are twins. The author didn't mention the Dionne quintuplets whose pictures had hung in her room for so long, but Marcella supposed that *five* spermatozoa must have sneaked in. By accident.

The book was as dumb as her biology text, they were alike, all full of illustrations and important words without really saying anything. "The velvety lining of the uterus," she read, "with its nourishing soft webbing of delicate blood vessels provides a warm secure haven for the fertilized ovum." Whatever that meant.

It turned out to mean the curse. The warm secure haven, which was full of blood vessels (so it was blood, after all, and not—what did her mother keep calling it?—discharge), was discarded every month, if there was no baby, and a new lining grew. So that—oh, the book didn't say so, but it was easy enough to figure out— if you were married, then each month you and your husband decided whether or not to plant a baby. If you didn't, then the lining came out. And if you did…

"Never Say Die" was a bore, all about how you were supposed to act on a date, how not to neck too much, all that stuff that Reverend Chettenforth was always lecturing about at Methodist Youth Fellowship. About how to behave at dances, which didn't matter anyway, Marcella never went to dances, her father wouldn't hear of it, there were only Saturday night shindigs at the Fall Valley roadhouse, and she was much too young to go there. Besides, serious Christians don't dance. Her interest flagged, she almost put the book down, but the title of the next chapter, "Peeping Through the Keyhole," stirred her curiosity… she wiggled back against the pillow, and read on.

"Peeping Through the Keyhole" was about masturbation. That was another word she'd never seen, so she had no idea what it meant. It made no sense, but she read on, because sometimes if you read long enough, you can figure out a new word.

She read the whole chapter clear through. It was a short chapter, and when Marcella finished, she had figured out that masturbation was wrong, whatever it was, and that it was like peeping through somebody's keyhole, like being a peeping tom, which everybody knows is terrible. But…mas – turb – a – tion. She'd never heard it spoken, and breaking it into parts didn't really help much. Sounded like it rhymed with men – stru – a tion. Sounded dirty, too. Maybe she could ask Cheryl what it meant, but Cheryl certainly didn't know, or she'd have said it by now.

Marcella read the chapter through again.

The only clue was in the next-to-the-last paragraph: "Many well-meaning parents used to tell their children that a continual practice of masturbation would cause insanity, or death, and although that piece of misinformation is still recorded in some otherwise informative books, nowadays we all agree that there is no such danger, and no need to frighten a young person so in order to make him stop. Perhaps it will help you if you think of it this way: masturbation by young people is like trying to peep through the keyhole on marriage, and while it is not physically harmful, prolonged masturbation can be psychologically debilitating. There is no question that it is entirely unnecessary and, in many cases, damaging in the way it misleads a young person, for the experience of sexual pleasure one person creates in solitude is not the same experience as mutually satisfactory coitus, shared by two people who deeply and genuinely love one another."

It was the part about sexual pleasure that bothered her. "Sexual pleasure one person creates in solitude…" was that what she'd been doing? Creating a sexual pleasure? She shook the notion away: it was too incredible. But the thought kept creeping back. There was no question that what she did, had done, was doing, continued to do every night, night after night, month after month—there was no question that it was pleasure. Sometimes she worried about that. About how much pleasure, maybe too much pleasure, maybe God doesn't like something that gives so much pleasure, but she always thrust that thought aside. Maybe...

She decided to reread the marriage chapter, because whatever masturbation is, it is not like marriage. But the marriage chapter was much too complicated to understand, despite its diagrams, and of course what she did wasn't at all like that. She'd never even seen an ovum, even though they come out every month, that's what Cheryl told her, and for a long time Marcella looked for one, white, she thought, on account of how eggs are white, but she hadn't known they would be so small—200 to an inch! No wonder she never found one, even though she watched carefully, thinking maybe she would spot one as it dropped into the toilet, but she never did, so she supposed that they drop out some other time, when she was asleep, or walking around, or sitting at her desk in school. She thought maybe ovums were the things that sometimes make your pants sticky for no reason, but that couldn't be right, because the stickiness happens more often than once a month and, besides, it looked a lot like the soppy white stuff that got all over her fingers when she...and sometimes her fingers weren't just wet, they were covered with something that looked like lather, and smelled, oh, sharp and sweet at the same time, but when she licked it once, it tasted mostly bitter, and then she thought maybe the ovum got all mixed up with that, and once a month came out, but she didn't notice it because everything was white.

Was that like peeping into marriage?

Ovums were sex things for sure, like kissing was, and menstruation, or they wouldn't be in the book, that's the reason they were there, just like the masturbation thing, and maybe, well, was what she kept doing a sex thing too? Pushing fingers way down to the baby place, pulling them out covered with white goop, and sometimes, even, once, with blood, because it was still her period, that was sort of a sex thing in itself, wasn't it, if periods are sex things? *Blood of the lamb.* And sex things are...

She scarcely dared think about it. She had not committed one single sin of commission, not once, since that awful day the summer after sixth grade when she went with Cheryl into the Catholic church, but this...if this was a sex thing, that would be a commission sin for sure, and an adult sin, besides, and the only sin worse than taking the name of the Lord thy God in vain, worse than cursing God, hadn't her mother said so? Because cursing is just cursing, and terrible, but sex things are disgusting, and filthy, and

She read the rest of the book, then went back to the beginning and reread it to the end, all about not necking, all about the ovum and spermatozoa, all about masturbation, all about periods, all about breasts, all about everything you need to know and what to do about it if you're growing up. And how to be proud without falling into pitfalls. But it was no use. Nothing helped her know for sure. The questions just kept rolling in her mind.

That afternoon Marcella looked up masturbation in the family dictionary, a hefty volume with worn thumb notches, but the word wasn't listed. Some other words were. *Coitus:* the natural conveying of semen to the female reproductive tract; sexual intercourse. *Sexual:* 1. of, relating to, or associated with sex, or the sexes. 2. having or involving sex. *Sex:* 1. either of two divisions or organisms distinguished respectively as male or female. 2. the sum of the structural, functional, and behavioral peculiarities of living beings that subserve reproduction by two interacting parents, and distinguish males and females. Intercourse meant something like talking, and coitus also meant coition, which meant copulation, which meant sexual intercourse, or coitus. That didn't help much.

Marcella walked downtown to the Hildreth Public Library, open Saturday afternoons from 2 to 4 o'clock, but Mrs. Rinde, the regular librarian, was on duty, so Marcella didn't dare sneak into the adult section. She might get caught looking at a grown-up sex book. The Young Adults shelves didn't have much, only books about blood cells in your body, and your bones, and one book about sex, but only about how babies are made.

She waited it out until Monday.

Monday, in study hall, after she'd finished her algebra assignment, she got permission to go into the high-school research library, the big one, with books for the whole county. Once there, she looked up masturbation in the card catalog. It wasn't listed. She looked up sex. Most of the sex books were in the 612.6 section. She memorized the number, then ruffled the cards up so they wouldn't fall open to sex the next time anyone opened up the Sa-Se drawer, and wandered down the long aisle of 600-680 books. Sure enough, right before the 613's was a whole *shelf* on sex, below engineering and inventions, and doctors and microbes, and above books about the brain, the eye, first aid, and water safety. And in between…whew! Dozens of them, some really old, all musty and crumbling, some newer. Even three medical books stacked up on the doctors and microbes shelf.

First she found a book on the brain that she could be studying for biology, and then she—furtively—began to pull out sex books, one at a time, looking up masturbation in the indexes. Lots of books listed it.

Reading everything took a long time. Marcella had to wait each day until her homework was done before she could get permission to leave the study hall, so some days she couldn't use the library. When she could, she often had to wait to make certain nobody was watching before she headed for the sex shelf. Then she had to find a book on the brain—or microbes—to be looking for, so she could pretend she'd picked the wrong book by accident if somebody surprised her.

It was slow going.

She had to look up so many words—androgen, estrogen, corpus luteum, colostrums—just to find the right place on the page. A sentence like "The follicle is converted into corpus luteum and begins to make progesterone which causes the uterine lining to thicken" turned out to be about periods, not about masturbation. "Dysmenorrhea" meant bad cramps.

As she looked up words, she learned a lot. Gestation (meaning pregnancy) lasts an average of 266 days, during which time a baby grows from one cell to more than 200 billion cells. If you cut open a breast, the inside looks like a cauliflower. She saw horrifying pictures of childbirth—sopping wet infants with large misshapen heads—and a diagram of a mother with one leg chopped off so you could see what happens when a child is born. But nothing stopped her from reading.

The more she read, the more frightened she became. Some old books said masturbation drives you crazy, some said a little bit wouldn't drive you crazy, but "excessive masturbation" would. Marcella was glad she'd read So You're Growing Up first. But even the new books agreed masturbation was terrible, although for different reasons: it hurt your soul, it made you secretive and not personable, it hurt your potency, it made you introverted, it gave you pimples. It was almost always listed in the "problems of sex" chapters—along with gonorrhea, syphilis, rape, homosexuality, and child molestation.

The more she read, the more confused she got. Masturbation seemed to be something only boys did. Yet she was certain…but at home that night, re-reading the book her mother had given her, she saw that, yes, the writer did only say "he," so maybe only boys could do it, maybe it was just another word for those emissions, but no, you were supposed to get used to the emissions, like breasts, but masturbation was something you were supposed to stop. Back in school, she re-examined the sex books. One after another, to her increasing relief, the masturbation sections said only "he" and "he"!

Then, as she teetered on the edge of dropping her research entirely, believing masturbation to be something women don't do, because they can't, she came across an old book with a long section written specifically about Women Masturbators, that was the title, about how Women Masturbators had been disgustingly known to gratify themselves by rubbing pillows back and forth between their legs. Back and forth, between.

Marcella felt a heavy flush creep up her neck. She slammed the book shut, sure that someone was watching her, but when she looked around, nobody was there. Her face and her head, oh, were swelling with such revulsion, and her stomach dropped, lower and lower, inside of her, in disgust and despair. There were, after all, women masturbators, and it did have something, then, somehow to do with things "down there," just as she feared, even though Marcella had never, disgustingly, put a pillow… But under the jumbled feelings, still lower, way in her deeps, no revulsion flickered, and no despair, but only the familiar rising and tingling that greeted her fingers each night as they tickled their way down her belly, beginning, oh, yes, beginning as soon as she'd read about the pillows, and how they rubbed…

When she got home, nobody was there. She took a pillow from the davenport downstairs, a pillow smaller, rounder, and firmer than the one she slept on. If she could produce those strange involuntary spasms that had been hers for so many months, if she could produce them by rubbing, and not by hunching against the headboard and letting her fingers drop deep in, if that is what the women masturbators disgustingly made happen, and if she *could*...then, at least, she would *know*.

She took the pillow upstairs and, leaving her panties on to catch the white lather, in case there was any, she straddled the pillow and began to rub.

How strange it felt.

First she stood, and rubbed, and the rubbing sent the tingling through her, oh, it did, just as her fingers sent the tingling. It went on, and on, and on. After a while she knelt beside the bed, because the book said they did it that way, and she rubbed and rubbed, at first gingerly, then more vigorously. The rubbing felt like a Kotex pad, when your pants pull too tightly, and it pushes way in. But nothing happened except more tingling. So she climbed in bed and, flat on her back like a beetle, she pushed the pillow back and forth, back and forth, trying harder and harder, straining, and holding her breath. She wiggled and pushed and arched her back, trying vainly to help things along, to settle the question, at least...

But the pillow rubbing was definitely not making any beautiful shuddering thing, none at all. It only increased the tingling, until her breath was bursting out of her in hot gushes, the tickling growing stronger and stronger, until finally she couldn't stand it a second longer.

It happened so quickly—flipping over on her stomach, the pillow bouncing off the bed and onto the floor, her back arching, her fingers flying under the barrier of her panties, their elastic tight and cutting her flesh, but not stopping, plunging, not caring, plunging, not thinking about anything at all, not about the pillow, or the Women, or even if she was making too much noise, until…oh, thank God, thank you glorious God oh my Father in heaven…rippling, and the spasms coming, hard and strong and throbbing all along the inside of her being…the spasms, again, and again.

Well, that settled nothing.

She checked the pillow carefully to make sure it wasn't soiled, then put it back on the davenport.

She hadn't found out, one way or the other. All she'd discovered was that she and the Women Masturbators eventually did different things, even though they started in the same general place. But that wasn't enough proof. She had to find out, specifically and clearly, whether or not…

So she kept exploring, and reading, in the secret shelf of the library. She learned the derivation of the word. It was from Latin—*manu*, meaning with the hand, and *stupare*, meaning to debauch. But debauch meant to seduce from chastity, which didn't make sense, but *manu*. That meant not only with pillows. She continued.

Then she found a description, at least she thought it was the same thing, and not just women did it… "Many girls discovered, in one fashion or another, that handling or other stimulation of the external genital region can cause a state of excitement usually accompanied by sexual thoughts. It is admittedly to a certain extent unnatural."

Handling, yes. Hands, yes. But external? And the sexual thoughts part didn't fit, either. She didn't think anything *sexual*, only about God, and sometimes she made up pictures of how her fingers must look, wandering, and exploring…

Until, at last, some time later, in a huge and unusually comprehensive book about sex, she found a description that was so detailed, and so localized, and with so many variations that, once she'd deciphered the meanings of all the words, there was no mistaking that she was, and she had been, "continually practicing masturbation."

❧ 12 ❧

It was not a simple question, oh Lord, no, it was not. There was the matter of sinning, of sinning a sin of commission, never mind how inadvertently, and there was the question of sinning the sin of sex, which is the filthy sin, the one God turns His face from in disgust, and there was the matter of adult sinning, and all three of these things, all three, done. Done. Done over and over, night after countless night, fingers flashing into...summer into fall and fall into winter and a year into another year, how many dozens of, hundreds of times, committed, *Father, forgive me, for I know not,* her words turning cold even as they left her mouth.

She had stumbled so many times. So many times, over and over, all the while thinking that she, Marcella, sinned only little sins, only sins of omission, tiny ones, not even telling dirty jokes—oh, sin of sex compounded by sin of pride!—and all the while fingers flashing, in, out, in, the very memory written huge across her blackened brain...where? where go, oh, and how forgive? how even request forgiveness, how beg...her fingers lathered with bitterness, veined with sorrow, her fingers, oh, pulled out and looked at, and still she had not *known*. How could she *not* have known?

If only she were a Catholic, but no, there was no Father to console her, and her own father, huge, and rough, what

would he do but make an ugly joke of it? or turn on her, angry…
no, impossible…and her mother? Her mother, stiff and cold,
unable to answer "what is menstruation, what does fuck mean,"
oh, no, her mother would never forgive her, even less than God—
God might not, but oh, her mother never would. But who could
help her then? Who?

Once she knew, there seemed to be no other choice.

So that Sunday, Marcella stayed after Methodist Youth
Fellowship, she stayed after the others had gone, although she
nearly lost her courage during Reverend Chettenforth's little talk
about "Fair Play with God." She nearly cried, listening: play fair
with God, and He'll play fair with you, but so many of us cheat…
not that she had cheated, of course she had not, but still barely
able to check her tears, sitting on the metal folding chair, trying
not to squirm in her distress, on the same chair used at ladies'
teas, at raising funds for African missions, and out again for
MYF, sitting still as stone, pulling her elbows in tight against her
body to hold her tears back, herself together, tightly pulling in
upon herself, waiting for Reverend Chettenforth to finish. Sitting
through his question and answer period. Silent. Asking nothing.
Listening. Trying to listen, to arguments about the genealogy of
Jesus, to the pros and cons of whether putting a handkerchief on
top of the Bible was a sin. The handkerchief discussion, which
Reverend Chettenforth kept encouraging, seemed endless.

And after that, the get-together: cookies, and Kool-Aid, and
everybody standing around asking what's the assignment for
World History, and have you done it yet, and are you going to the
game Monday night, and some of them slowly pairing off, like
she had done with Bobby, drifting out the door, on their way to
walking home. Marcella, waiting, watching them go, one by one,
staying as though it was her turn to help clean up, and finally,
when everybody was gone, saying…saying nothing, nothing

at all, not knowing how to say it, what to say, not knowing if Reverend Chettenforth had ever heard about this sin she would have to make up to God for, not knowing if he'd ever heard the word before. If he were a priest, he'd know, of course, because priests have to listen to all sorts of things, there is nothing too base for them to listen to, but Reverend Chettenforth?

Clearing her throat, she finally broached the subject, speaking in words that felt as large as watermelons, but sounded as if she were merely inquiring about the propriety of placing a hanky on top of the Bible:

"Reverend Chettenforth, do you know about masturbation?" She pronounced it just like the dictionary said to, with a short "a," a long "a," and the accent on the third syllable. It was the first time she'd heard the word spoken.

Reverend Chettenforth apparently knew. There was a perceptible stiffening in his limbs, even though he continued to stack hymnals on the table. Then he turned and, taking care not to look directly at Marcella, replied: "Yes, I know about it. What makes you ask?"

Marcella's words came tumbling out, her face flushed behind them: "Because, well, because, you see, I..." But before she could continue a confession that, Reverend Chettenforth told himself, she could only regret later, he held up his hand and began his monologue:

"God put us here upon His earth so that we might procreate, and provide vessels for His living souls. He gave us our sexual drives for a reason, and for a purpose, a holy purpose. And God did not intend that we should use these drives for any lesser design." His words began rolling off his tongue, as he warmed to his subject.

"That is the lesson taught to us by the Garden of Eden: for in that time, man did not yet know what it was to spill his seed, for

God made Eve out of a rib of Adam, and in doing so, He gave to us, He gave to mankind, He gave to our ancestors a chance to live out untold lifetimes in eternity."

But no! But no! Reverend Chettenforth did not understand! Marcella half-reached toward him in an attempt to interrupt. But the minister went on without a pause, his eyes still avoiding hers as he spoke.

"For God is a just God. It is we who are weak and frail. We are the sinners; we are all sinners, we were born in sin, we have lived in sin ever since Eve did give of the apple to eat, we are all sinners ever since the moment Adam did bite. God gave Adam a chance, oh, yes, He gave Adam a chance for all mankind to live forever in paradise, but Adam was weak, like you and I, and could not rise above his weakness."

But. But. Marcella felt frantic. He must think that she...oh! That she was ignorant of the *sin* of masturbation. She knew! She knew! But his big words were as confusing as the terms in those medical books, still, he wouldn't mention Adam unless he meant sin, and she had meant...no!

"If Adam had been strong, if he had been blessed with the strength of a purer man, we would still be living in a state of grace...do you understand?" Marcella, tumultuous inside, could only nod, dumbly. "But Adam did eat of the apple, and he did sin. And God turned him out of the Garden. From that moment, from the moment the Lord sent His angels to guard the gate, from that moment was all fleshly lust born. For that was part of the choice: so Eve bore Cain, and she bore Abel, and she bore in pain, as all others of the earth have since born in pain, and that is part of duty. We chose to be expelled from the Garden, and so we must now procreate in lust, and bear in pain..."

"But —," Marcella cried. It was no use. He did not understand that she knew the sin, she knew the sinning and please dear God by all that is Holy would sin no more! Oh, that was not even the question. As though she might repeat? Never! How could she? How would she dare? That would be as though Eve had returned to the Garden, as though Eve had sinned a small sin and been allowed to return to the Garden and not thrust out into this purgatory of a world, as though she had gone right back and done it again: Here. Take, eat, this is my apple...No! No! Marcella *never* would have, she *never* would have taken that apple when God had said, of any fruit may you eat but this one.

"These are not easy things," Reverend Chettenforth continued, misinterpreting Marcella's interruption. "But God is a just God, and He provided us with the means for working ourselves out of the sin of Adam and into the state of grace, through Jesus Christ our Lord, of course, but not without pain. Not even His Son avoided pain.

"So that any man who violates the law of procreation, any man who refuses to know his wife, any man and wife who refuse to bless their union with children, such people are as Eve, offering once again the apple to eat; such people are as Adam, taking, and eating, and sinning the sin of disobedience as well. For did not God Himself admonish us: thou shalt not spill thy seed?

"So go, my child, and sin no more."

Reflecting, only after he saw Marcella's bewildered face, that his lecture had, after all, been devised with young men in mind. Strange he had not noticed that before. Perhaps he should create a new lesson...but now, no more could he do. Truth is truth, regardless of its biology. Turning, back to the table, he began stacking the hymnals, signaling the end of the conversation.

But she hadn't known! She hadn't known! It was as though God had put Adam and Eve into the Garden and had said *nothing* to them, of *course* she would not sin again...go, and sin no more, that was not the question...God had not said to her, eat not, or maybe He had said eat not, but she hadn't heard Him, not until now, and now, outside the gates, and angels with their fiery swords guarding against her return, and how, oh, how effect a return, through fire and sword, how—*that* was the question.

Words falling out of her mouth, flat, when she tried to pray, nothing but words, tumbling to the floor, not even rising to Heaven. Christ, her beloved Christ of the Garden, she had not seen Him for days! And the music, even the music—oh, she tried, but the music brought her no closer, no, no closer to God than if she were dancing, instead of lamenting...but that was the very trouble: how to approach a great and just God, how to make one's voice rise to Heaven, weighted with this enormous guilt, this unbelievably gigantic burden of not once, not twice, not three times eating—but dozens, and *hundreds,* and maybe even THOUSANDS of times SINNING

To such a panic that her voice, when she finally found it, came out much higher, and much louder, than she had intended, sounding more like a wail than a query, halting Reverend Chettenforth as he walked, with his arms full of hymnals, to the storage room; to such a panic that her words, unable to sustain the load of questioning that her mind bore, exploded into only: "But what shall I *do?*"

Her cry echoed through the basement room, reverberating with her desire to absolve herself of the formidable weight her guilt had become. Reverend Chettenforth, however, heard none of that, he heard only "how can I stop masturbating." Her words conveyed nothing to him of her frozen and frantic concern to reach her God, to absolve herself of this formidable weight.

But to little difference. For even if he had understood, his response most certainly would have been the same: to turn, to pause, and—staring doggedly out from under wrinkled brows—to say: "What is there to do, Marcella, but pray. And persevere." She watched his back disappear into the storage closet.

❧ 13 ❧

It was the most difficult letter Marcella had ever written in her whole life. She rewrote it endlessly, trying out sentences this way and that, despairing. How could she ever say it? Asking Reverend Chettenforth had been bad enough.

Hildreth, Kansas
October 12, 1947

Dear Brother Morgan,

She remembered him the way he looked when he preached that day, tall and lean and tanned. She pictured him standing with a red hymnal in his hands, his head thrown back, singing.

I am writing to you because you converted me (June 6, 1945, Hildreth Evangelical United Brethren Church)

Meticulously she copied the particulars out of her white Testament, in case Brother Morgan wanted to look it up

and I don't know who else to talk to. I already tried talking to my minister, Reverend Chettenforth, but that didn't help much.

She couldn't decide whether to leave the last sentence in or not. She erased it, wrote it again, erased it. Finally she left it. The hardest part was still ahead:

My problem is that I've been practicing masturbation for a long time now, only I didn't know what a sin it was when I began, or I would have stopped right then. In fact, I did stop, as soon as I found out it was wrong, and I haven't done it since, for more than a week now, but my problem is this:

She knew Miss Patterson, her English teacher, would call that paragraph wordy, but she couldn't think of a shorter way to say it.

When I try to pray to God about it, I don't think He's listening. I mean, before, when I prayed, I got a certain feeling after my prayer that let me know everything was okay, and I could go on from there. But this thing I was doing is so awful, I don't even know how to pray about it, or what to do for God so He'll forgive me. Can you help me? Or can you recommend someone who can?

She copied the last sentence out of her typing manual, to make the letter sound more grown-up.

Yours in the Lord,
Marcella Colby

The idea to write to Brother Morgan had leaped into her mind a few days after her talk with Reverend Chettenforth. Once she thought of him, she didn't understand why she hadn't thought of him before. He was the perfect person to turn to, a man of God, yet far enough away so he couldn't be embarrassed knowing her.

But once the letter was mailed. Marcella began to worry. What if Brother Morgan was too disgusted to answer her letter? What if he wrote to Reverend Chettenforth about her? Or to her mother? What if Lucille saw his answer, and began teasing her about love letters? Or if Mrs. Colby broke her longstanding rule about never opening other people's mail and found out about everything?

Brother Morgan's reply, though, came winging in on Evangelical Church stationery, looking so official that Mrs. Colby wasn't even curious. "Here. Some sort of church literature for you," was all she said.

And oh, what relief that he'd actually answered! Oh, what blessing…

> *Midwestern Council*
> *Evangelical Church*
> *Denver, Colorado*
> *October 16, 1947*

Dear Marcella,

Be cheerful, my little chickadee. Even God does not like long faces. Besides, everything comes out in the wash—even the buttons, sometimes! So let the sunshine be your guide. More, later, when I can find the time.

(Please excuse this writing—I have a hand like a foot.)

> *In His service,*
> *Big Jim*

Marcella had forgotten what a joker he was—and he didn't even sign it Brother Morgan!

"Miracle of miracles," she wrote in her diary, "he really answered me. I am not alone. God is my strength and my salvation."

She used a kind of code in her diary—not that Mrs. Colby would read it. She left Marcella's things alone. But Lucille was not to be trusted. Lucille read her diary once, and found some love poems about Tommy Edwards, and she told him about them, oh! What shame that caused Marcella, all the worse because Tommy was Cheryl's boyfriend, well, not boyfriend, exactly, but Cheryl had liked him first, before Marcella.

October 19, 1947

Dear Big Jim,

I guess it's okay to call you Big Jim, because that is how you signed your letter. You don't know how much good your letter did me, it really did. I went around the house singing all day, and last night, when I prayed, well, it still wasn't like it used to be, but not as bad as before. I get the feeling that at least God is listening, now. Thank you, thank you, thank you.

The Lord's daughter,
Marcella

His reply came almost immediately.

Denver, Colorado
October 21, 1947

Dear Pumpkin,

You can call me anything you like. That's what I tell everyone— even my wife, and you should hear some of the things she calls me!

Know why God created Adam first? So he could get a word in edgewise! How's this one: Adam blamed Eve, Eve blamed the serpent, and the serpent didn't have a leg to stand on.

Seriously, keep up the good work. Will try to write more when I'm not so busy. (Remember, a corn on the ear is worth two on the foot.)

Yours until Niagara Falls,
Yosemite Jim

Well, things went a lot easier after that, even though Brother Morgan hadn't given her any real advice. Not that God always seemed closer. Or even listening. He didn't. But whenever He seemed too far away, Marcella imagined Big Jim in his white robe, singing hymns, or cracking silly jokes, and the thought was enough to cheer her on. Finally she was able to write:

October 23, 1947

Dear Big J.,

I have good news. I've been praying, you know, morning and night even before I began writing to you—praying and crying before I got your letter, and then not crying so much afterwards, because of what you said about sunshine. And then I wrote (remember?) about how I thought God was listening again?

Well, the other night, I got down on my knees like I have been, every night, at bedtime, and I was just praying there, and trying very hard not to think about some of the other things I have done on my knees beside the bed (you will know what I mean from my first letter, if you don't understand from this one), and I was feeling so badly, remembering how I'd sinned, but I kept trying not to think about that part, but only about God, and how much He loves us all, maybe even me, and guess what happened? I started hearing "In the Garden." (Do you sing it in the Evangelical Church, too?) That's the melody I always hear when I know that everything is okay between God and me again, and then I really did start crying, only tears of happiness, that He had heard me, and that He had answered. And then I thought I actually heard His voice, inside of me, saying, "Marcella, you are forgiven. Go, now, and sin no more." So of course I promised Him that I wouldn't ever again. I mean I made that promise before, when I discovered what I was doing, and I haven't fallen since, only maybe once or twice at first when I still wasn't sure what I was doing, but this promise is different, because I know God's love is surrounding me again, and He is hearing everything in my heart. I try to make it sunshine like you said. Oh, it is so good! It is so good! Thank you, thank you, thank you.

Your Kansas sunflower,
Marcella

But things weren't quite that simple. Going to bed, for instance...it was getting risky, going to bed. Marcella would climb in, and stretch her legs, and before she even had time to think about it, she would be tickling—oh! Keeping her promise was hard! That surprised her. She decided to stay up later and get really sleepy, which she often did, nodding over a book until Mrs. Colby nudged her upstairs. That helped some. But if she forgot, and climbed in bed before she was really tired, the temptation seemed to increase. "Do you think it's God's way of testing me, to see if I mean what I say?" she wrote Big Jim.

There were other signs. Like the day in school, sitting on the flat wooden assembly-hall seats, trying to study and feeling... something...sort of delicate pinpricks down there, shooting nearly as high as her stomach, then prickling so hard it was pain, or near pain, as she tensed herself against the sensation, how dare she, here, in public...fighting it, pushing it away, until she slowly realized that she was only feeling her underpants pulling in against her. That shocked her. She resolved to be more careful.

And the day her bicycle, that old tin-fendered, bought-during-the-war bicycle—how could it turn on her? But it did, it did, the tongue of its narrow seat rubbing, rubbing, as her pumping legs rotated her body down, down, over and over...she was already breathing heavy when she noticed...and then, leaping clear of the temptation, how disgusting! like she was a woman masturbator with a pillow between her legs. ("Have I come to that?" she cried into her diary later, carefully not specifying what "that" was.)

Shaking her blue jeans loose but, wary, standing up to pump her way home, even though the sensations had ebbed. She parked the bike permanently in the garage. She began to worry.

"You don't think I'll give in to it, do you?" she wrote Jim.

"Think of it as an itch you can't reach," he replied, "the sort of itch that you get under a cast if you break your arm."

She tried. But the itch wanted scratching all the time. She thought about wearing mittens full of oatmeal to bed, like Lucille had to when she had the chicken pox so she wouldn't scratch the scabs, but how could she explain that to Mrs. Colby?

Still, the letters helped. Sometimes they helped a lot, for a couple of days, even, before she'd find herself back where she'd started. Not scratching, she discovered, wasn't so hard during the day. She had plenty then to keep herself busy, with school, and the organ lessons, and the church meetings she attended. Nighttime was the real test. If she wasn't thinking, sometimes her hands would move, down, down, toying with the elastic of her pajama pants, toying and sometimes—*Dear God, please forgive me*—tugging at the elastic, pulling, pulling, pajama bottoms riding up high, catching in the crack place, the cloth jerking into, and into...

Sometimes she had to grip her headboard to keep from doing it.

Or pull herself out of bed to write another letter.

"Writing to you helps," she told Jim, "not that I think I'd ever do it again, but just the same, it does get pretty difficult sometimes, resisting." Because she had to resist. She couldn't believe it was true, but it was.

When it happened, it happened in the morning. That was unexpected. She was used to struggling at night, but not in the morning and waking, this morning, slowly, no, not waking but only rousing, half-aware that the thin morning light was beginning to fill her room, half-aware that her parents' alarm had not yet rung, that it was early. The morning air felt chilly, thermostat still down, nobody up yet, no need to get up...She stretched, under the bedclothes, her body's heat in a central cluster, warm limbs striking against cold sheets. So nice, in bed. Music meandered in her mind. *O God our help in a – ges past, Our hope for years to come,* relaxing into it, floating on it, letting her mind wander through its layers.

It was as if she hadn't really wakened, into the here and now, but only roused into that no-time place between, so she wasn't thinking about it at all, that's how it happened. She wasn't even thinking about it, only about whether or not to get up now, or to roll around and sleep some more instead, and she decided to sleep, not even thinking that there might be a reason to get up. So she didn't. She just rolled over, on her stomach, and wiggled around some, to get comfortable, and somehow, she guessed her arm must have slid down along her side when she rolled over, and she wasn't exactly on her stomach, but sort of half there, so that her hand had room to slip into her pajama bottoms easily enough, and she was still half asleep, really, or she would have recognized what she was doing.

But she wasn't even thinking about it, only about how cool the sheets were, and how warm her body, and how gentle her hands, stroking, stroking. Stroking, and stroking. She wasn't thinking, and her hands, when she felt them moving over her body, didn't remind her of anything bad, they felt as innocent as they used to, soft, and smooth, stroking, stroking, pulling her back and back in time, until she couldn't begin to think who she was, or what she was doing: if she had thought, she never would have done it, not in a thousand years. But she wasn't thinking, really, she hadn't even fully wakened, and she dropped down, down, like she used to, into the music, fingers tickling body, fingers dropping, fingers pushing, gently, in…and when it happened, it happened so fast, one moment half asleep and the next moment, *doing* it, oh, good merciful Lord in Heaven, not even realizing what it was that she was doing, not understanding what had come over her, until…The realization came like a sharp explosion in her body that burst one horrified portion of her brain wide awake: *Oh, my God, what are you doing, Marcella, whatever are you doing?*

And knowing, then, the doing. *Oh, dear God in Heaven,* her fingers pressing, probing, down deep, *what are you doing,* pushing, shoving, *who do you think you are,* flopping on her stomach, then, and not just halfway, *Mar – cel – la!* her words swelling to a scream within her head while her body

It was as though her body became, for the moment, a totally separate thing, as though her body, writhing on the bed, had a will of its own. Resisting for so long had left her so vulnerable, she did not even have to lift up her haunches—her inner flesh flashing through its stages, from incredible softness to a tightness like the string of a mandolin, her fingers tuning it, and tuning, until the tightness turned to hardness before…*bursting*

The spasms, the shudders, pressing down upon her, such strong ones, there was no denying them, they burst upon her with such force, she was a flag flapping in a gale, the force breaking through her again, and again. There was no question of stopping.

After the storm was quite spent, yearnings wafted over her, over her whole being, yearnings, so strong, it was as though she hadn't done what she'd just finished doing, it was as though she hadn't done it at all, but she had! she had! And in her sorrow, and her fright, and her anger, she let herself, she made herself, yes, now, there, *do it!* she jammed her fingers right back, yes, there, *inside!* and, she did it, again, and again, once more trembling, yes, again, panting, heaving, quaking, *oh, God forgive!* until she could no longer tell when that shuddering stopped, and the shuddering from her anguished crying began.

Several days passed before she could wrench herself out of her shame long enough to write to Big Jim. She cried as she wrote, *Oh, dear Jim,* believing that he could never write to her again after receiving this letter, but driven by a scrupulous honesty, *I don't know how to write this to you, because I am so ashamed, but I masturbated again. Wednesday morning. God tested me, and I failed.*

Brother Morgan's reply was brief, but never had he written so directly:

November 23rd

Dear Marcella,

It's a tough go, kid, but you can lick it. I know you can. Let me hear how you do.

Yours until butter flies,
Uncle Jim

The struggle never really eased after that.

Marcella tried harder than ever to keep busy, playing the piano for hours on "bad" days, practicing the scales, the Czerny exercises, the John Thompson pieces. When her folks couldn't bear to listen to her one second longer, she would walk over to the church and practice the organ, untangling the mysteries of the double-tiered keyboard and the heavy foot pedals. She memorized hymns, picking out the melodies, and then the chording. She could play a number of pieces, even some difficult ones, fast enough for singing. If only she could keep her hands occupied…but it would creep upon her in the most incongruous places. She would be brushing her teeth, scrubbing away, and squinting at her new face in the mirror, getting older, older, every day, every day a different face (her biology teacher told them how your skin is always dying), and watching her toothbrush go down, down, down, and not across, not even noticing…her mound, pushed hard against the cold porcelain corner of the sink, not even realizing…rotating, rotating, ever so gently to the brushing of her teeth, rotating, until

Oh no! not again! Dear God dressing rapidly, fumbling, *please forgive,* pulling clothes into place, *I am so sorry,* and downstairs to

Safety in the kitchen, home free, king's X, sitting—temporarily immune—beside her mother, beside Lucille, and neither of them knowing, neither suspecting, and as soon as she began to think that those feelings had disappeared altogether, the thought flashed across her brain: what would they dear God in heaven think if she just reached down and stuck her hand inside her panties, stuck it down and *up* and…

Not being alone was one of her rules. She had a list of them:
1. Keep hands busy
2. Make sure you're not alone
3. Don't think about it

That last one was tough. Keeping her mind off of it was just about the hardest thing she could do. She thought about it nearly all the time, except sometimes, she didn't think about it when she should, like the time Bobby Coleman wanted to walk her home, again, after MYF, and she let him. He kissed her.

April 6, 1948

Dear Big Jim,

I think kissing makes it harder. I never thought about that before, but I think it's true. Not that I kiss much, I don't, but the other

night, my old boyfriend asked to walk me home from MYF. It was right during a time when I was having a big battle, not doing it. Anyway, I let him, and we kissed (I don't NECK, of course!!!!), but I let him hold my hand on the way home, and then he wanted to kiss me, so I just thought I'd try it, but kissing him made it harder, I think, though I haven't figured out why yet, except that afterwards, when I came in, my body felt hot all over, like I was blushing or something, and then it was so difficult, not doing it. I mean even though I was praying and everything, it was not easy to keep my hands off myself. Well, I just couldn't. So I'm thinking that maybe I shouldn't kiss anymore. Like maybe, if I have a date, I shouldn't let him kiss me goodnight, even. Or maybe not hold hands? I think that's where the trouble began, but I couldn't tell for sure...

The longer she managed to resist doing it, the more horrible it seemed when at last...and she would find herself doing awful things, like standing up! Or on her knees, even, oh, much worse than if she'd given in earlier, the regular way, in bed...and once in the bathroom, sitting on the toilet, reading, not even thinking about it, just reading, and stroking her thigh, not noticing what she was doing when suddenly, before she could even realize... her fingers! Flashing up inside her...and thinking, my God, but if I'm going to do it, I should at least have the decency to go back to my room and lie down

but too late. She had already crossed the line. There was a line that, well, once she crossed, it was almost impossible to stop and already *oh, NO!*

crossing, and she nearly giggled at the thought of herself doing it sitting up, how could she? Such a heinous sin, still, oh, sitting on the toilet with her eyes squinched shut (she always squinched her eyes shut, she didn't know why) and with her finger, *oh dear God, please,* jerking in and out and in again, *oh, no,* until, finally, stretching her body up, out, almost in a straight line, like push-ups in gym class, only backwards, thrusting her stomach way up into the tile-contained air, before she could

actually manage, oh, Jesus Christ, holy Mary Mother of God, *somebody* help me *stop* until, not able to hold herself erect, oh! Collapsing on the toilet, still quivering

May 15, 1948
Oh, Jim, sometimes I think I am the most despicable person in the whole world!

She wondered if God loved her anymore. How could He, she asked herself. How could He love me, even me, I have broken so many promises to Him, I have broken so many promises, so many resolutions, it isn't that I want to

And she prayed to Him, sometimes for hours on "bad" days, or in the evenings, or on Saturday afternoons when she didn't have anything else to do. Lucille teased her all the time. "Goody-goody," she taunted, "you'll wear the skin off your knees that way." But Marcella didn't care. She prayed for Lucille. She felt sorry for her, almost thirteen years old and still not saved, why hadn't God revealed Himself to her? But Marcella knew He hadn't, because she'd heard Lucille lie to her mother about her girlfriends. "Nice girls," she said, but they weren't. They were fast girls, wearing lipstick on the sly and everything, even teasing boys. "Dear God," she prayed, "let Lucille see the error of her ways." Then she would chronicle her own sins, one by one, for the past week, or two weeks, and "that" sin always led the rest. She begged forgiveness, and promised, promised, never ever ever to do it again, but sometimes when she got up from her praying, well, sometimes praying too much about it seemed almost as bad as thinking too much about it, so sometimes when she got up, she found that she couldn't resist any longer, and she would do it, not there, not where she'd been praying, for goodness sake, but after, soon enough after to throw herself back into boundless grief, but sometimes she rose from her prayers feeling that the slate really had been wiped clean again, and she could almost see it, without a single mark, and on those days her exhilaration—like her earlier despair—knew no limits.

June 3, 1948

Dearest Jim, the bad part is all over now. I can tell. I get up in the morning, smiling, and full of sunshine, and I pray to Him who lights my golden days, and sometimes I cry, tears of happiness that He in His mercy could forgive a sinner like me, but that is all over. That is all over and behind me now, and I can get up in the morning, and smile, and be free for loving Him who loves me so much. And at night, I drop to my knees once more, and send up my special prayers to Him, prayers of thanks, that He in His wisdom chose to reveal Himself to me through you, so I could turn to you in my need, and so you could answer me. And I pray to Him to watch over you, which I know He does, of course, you being not only such a good Christian, but also important in the church, and sometimes I pray to Him to send you back out to Hildreth so I can see you again, but I know how busy you are, and always I pray for a few extra angels to watch over you, because of everything you've done for me. I don't know what I would have done without you. Whenever I needed you most, you were there. You know what I mean. I can't say these things too well...

Then, only days after she mailed the letter, she did it *again,* just when she was certain she had it licked. She was crushed. She even started to think that if this kept up, she would have to kill herself, there would be nothing else left to do. But oh, no, how could she think that? Suicide is as wicked a sin as murder, that's what suicide is, anyway, killing yourself. No, she must see it through, somehow. But then she caught herself thinking maybe she should chop her hands off, that would do it—whap, whap, like Mrs. Schnieder's chickens, fountains of blood spurting from her arm stubs, or maybe here's what she'd do (she couldn't believe she was really thinking these things) chop one finger off every time she fell. She saw herself, fingers, thumbs, all gone, wearing gloves stuffed with sawdust, flapping like a scarecrow in the breeze...Her laughter made her feel even worse, how could she joke about such a thing? But before she could write Jim about her newest depravity, she received another letter:

June 8, 1948

Dear Cutie Pie (or is it Pie Cutter?),

No more pencils, no more books, eh? How does it feel to be out of the sweat shop for a while? Your old Uncle Jim is going to get away from it all, too. Going to scale a Rocky Mountain top, get me a breath of fresh air. See some stars again. May and I are going to run the Evangelical's Western Mountain Camp this summer. Say, why don't you come? I'll bet you can. Doesn't cost much, and there'll be lots of kids. I'll stick a brochure in here, with time, place, cost, how many toothbrushes to bring, all that stuff. Ask your mother. See if you can come gambol with us mountain goats.

To boys 'n' berries,
Big Jim

It was the answer to her prayers.

❧ 14 ❧

Her folks had really let her go, was it true? But here she was, on the Greyhound bus, jogging her way across the state of Kansas, and into Colorado—oh, mountains! and Jim! She was going to see him again, could it be? She had been so afraid they wouldn't let her come. When she asked, her mother said no, she was much too young to go so far away from home, and her father, oh! he hadn't liked the idea one bit.

"What do you need to go gallivanting around the country for?" he asked her angrily. "And who is this Jim anyway? What do you have in mind to do, up there, in those mountains? Writing to someone behind our backs, how can we trust you any more?"

But here she was. Reverend Chettenforth finally had convinced them. She could never thank him enough, maybe he knew how good this would be for her. She tried to imagine what it would be like: Big Jim in his white robe, the mountains, was she really going to see mountains for the first time in her whole life, and the kids, what kind of kids would be there? Not like the kids in Hildreth, she hoped, getting snootier and snootier every day, and just because she was trying to be a good Christian, what was wrong with that, they were really ashamed of themselves, she bet, but maybe, maybe she could make a camp friend? Oh, but that was asking too much, why would she need a friend, she would have Big Jim, but just the same, another girl would be nice, someone her own age, not all the time tempting her like Cheryl had, but Christian. She wondered if they would be. Or if they would be heathens, sent by their ministers and their parents in the hopes that they'd get saved. And she, Marcella, and Big Jim, the only ones there who knew the love of God personally, oh, of course, he knowing it so much better than she, but helping her. Teaching her how to save souls. If only she could sing like May. But maybe she could play the piano for him, if they had a piano. What would it be like, anyway? Just tents and things?

The bus swayed down the two-lane highway, slowed to trail behind a farm truck, then picked up speed again. The country still looked the same as when she left Hildreth, cornfields stretching out every which way, the tassled tops already turned the color of burnt sugar.

It was the first time Marcella had ever traveled alone, but she wasn't scared, hardly at all, there was nothing to be scared of, her parents put her on the bus, Big Jim would meet her, and here she was, riding along like this. She kept thinking of her father, and how mad he'd gotten, the tendons on his neck bulging as he argued with her mother, "Nothing but a spoiled brat, that's all." Still, they had let her come. Soon she would be—oh, when? when? Big Jim waiting to meet her. She couldn't help thinking he already was waiting, that he'd been waiting for her all the time she was riding the bus, that he was standing up in the mountains, looking down the road, watching for her bus, like she was watching out the window, for the mountains, for him…but there was nothing to see, only power lines stringing out above the speckled fields. Only telephone poles snapping by, blap, blap, blap, blap. They made her dizzy.

She unpacked her lunch and ate: a bologna sandwich and a banana. She wished she'd brought something to wash it down. Finally she dozed, the slick glass of the window cool against her skin.

She woke to a green-and-white Quaker Motor Oil sign, and a long silver strip of railroad track running alongside the road. She couldn't remember where she was at first, then she did, and looked for the mountains. There were none, but the land had changed. No more dead tree trunks, stripped naked and raw of bark. No more puffs of dust signaling some farmer on his tractor. No more windmills. That was behind them. Here was—sage brush. The beginnings of, yes, really—hills! And a Coor's beer sign. Made in Colorado. She was really there.

Oh, how much farther?

She stuck her hand in her purse to feel the white Testament she'd brought with her. *I come to the gar – den a – lone.* She pulled it out and stroked its pebbly cover. Oh, Jim would be so good for her, she knew he would. *And the voice I hear...* He would teach her, so many things. How to pray, really pray, like a minister does, and how to draw closer to God, how to ask His blessing. Maybe he could even explain to her how you know whether or not something is God's will. That was always so confusing. She couldn't begin to figure it out. Oh, she thought she had, once, before, when she counted on God's hymns welling up to tell her, but look where that had led her. Would he—she pulled her Bible tight against her—when he met her, would he, you know, look funny at her because of what she'd written? Oh, she sincerely hoped not.

But they would talk about it, of course, she could see them now, they would talk, all quiet, and pray, like they had prayed together on her conversion day, when she'd come down the aisle, felt the weight of his warm hands on her head, and she kneeling, and his beautiful voice above her, praying. Maybe he would ask forgiveness for her: Dear God, forgive this little child of yours— oh surely goodness and mercy he would, and she would draw such courage, she knew it, so much courage from being with him that she would never even *want* to do it again.

She had started to drift to sleep when the bus rounded a bend, and suddenly, there stood mountains, in a row, still far away, but definitely not hills, she could see the white that must be snow cresting them. Oh, where had they come from? Was Jim in them, somewhere up there? She pressed her head hard, hard, against the glass. So different from the pictures. Bigger, of course, she had expected that, so big they made the road ahead look like a curl from a cigarette pack. But so much more beautiful, too, the sandy foothills edged with silver-green rising to blend into deep forest tones, to the grays of glacial rock, to blues, to—oh! for *pur – ple moun – tain maj – es – ties*, it wasn't just a song, they really *were* purple.

She grew thirsty again, she'd been riding so long. They must be almost there.

But they weren't. The bus kept rolling along the curving blacktop, pushing farther and farther into the range until they were inside it. Close up, the mountains seemed even more majestic, more beautiful. Still, there was something...she looked, and looked. Then slowly she knew. They were deep, so deep, as though the mountains that she saw were only tips— they had to be—like icebergs, showing only a fraction of their whole, as though they were rooted, oh, who could know how deep? The thought made her stomach feel queer. She couldn't begin to imagine how far down they must plunge. But there was no mistaking it, the mountains were much more than what she could see.

She watched, like one hypnotized, as the huge masses of land slowly metamorphosed into floating shapes in the twilight. She watched them darken, not so much to black as to a deep purple, their peaks swollen against the sky. She stared and stared until the shapes grew indistinct, wispy as smoke, until she could see them no more, not even a hint, until all she could see were the headlights pressing a beam against the immense black night, only speed-limit signs and lane markers glistening back, eerie phosphorescent shapes.

But she knew the mountains remained. She could feel them, making the night so different from nights back home—the mountains, everywhere, surrounding her, enclosing her, embracing her, yet at the same time distant, impenetrable, diminishing her. She could sense them standing all around her, thrusting up, and up, and up, *Fa – ther all glo – ri – ous, O'er all vic – to – ri – ous,* and descending to—oh, descending to—she dared not imagine what core.

Meeting Jim was a lot different than she'd expected. She spotted him first, she was sure it was Jim, standing in the neon-lit street, right under a flashing luncheonette sign. Wearing a T-shirt. And khaki pants! But he was stockier than she remembered, his hair shorter, his head more massive on his shoulders—maybe he was the wrong man? Standing, his eyes scanning the clutter of people getting off the bus.

"Brother Morgan?" she asked, feeling suddenly timid.

"Marcella!" he said, hardly giving her time to nod before he had her baggage check and was shuffling through the suitcases.

He was enormously big, close up, more like a football player than a minister.

"Cheryl wanted to see me off, but I said no, because of my folks being there." Marcella was babbling. She hadn't seen Cheryl for weeks, not since school let out, and besides, Jim didn't know her. "There," she finally managed, pointing. It was her father's suitcase, Mr. Colby had let her use it. Jim tossed it in the back of a ramshackle station wagon.

"Meet Betsy," he said, patting the car. "Hop in."

They edged out to the highway, drove a bit, Jim talking and joking. Then they turned off, onto a narrow road that seemed to lead straight up.

"Old Betsy will never make it up this hill unless we cross our fingers, cutie pie. I can call you that, can't I? That won't embarrass you, will it?"

Marcella squirmed but smiled, uncertain how to take this attention.

"She didn't say no," Jim told the car. "Wouldn't matter if she did say no. Girls don't mean no when they say no, anyway, do they, Betsy? What's that old saw? When a lady says no, she means maybe; when she says maybe, she means yes; when she says yes, she's no lady. Betsy should know. You're always the lady, aren't you, Betsy? Hey!" The car dropped over the top of the hill, then around a hairpin curve. "Don't fall out!" Jim shouted in mock alarm, and then, with no warning, "So tell me, my little pumpkin, how are things going with you? You haven't written your old Uncle in nearly a week."

What to say. She hadn't expected that he, here, and especially right now, when they'd been together maybe ten minutes, in the middle of his joking and everything, she hadn't expected him to ask. She sat twisting her dress, without noticing.

"What's the matter, cat got your tongue?"

But it was so hard to speak about it, she'd never thought they'd talk about it right away, oh certainly later, but not yet, not here, how much easier, writing, but here he was sitting in the car beside her, and alone, they were all alone, and that was difficult enough, by itself, she was glad the night hid her face, all alone with a man,

"It gets harder, if I date," she remembered writing him, but must say something, or he'll…

"No, I, well, everything's like before, you know, I try, I really try to stop it, and sometimes, a week goes by before I…but I pray, like you said, and ask forgive—"

She felt herself drawing close to tears trying to talk about it this way, in the front seat of a station wagon, bouncing along some mountain road. She had to stop it.

"But last week, well, I was so excited about coming here and everything and so much to do. It's always easier, you know, when I'm busy, and then I don't get such…well, those feelings, you know, they don't come so often, so it isn't so hard."

Finally she was able to move her head enough to take a peek at him. He was silent, driving the car, both hands on the steering wheel, his eyes ahead. On the road. The dashboard lights showed the hair on his hands. Marcella felt better; she stirred a bit.

"Oh, it'll be better this week, you'll see," she said. "So much to do, and you right here, I've been writing so many letters to you, and now you, right here. It'll be no problem at all. I don't begin to know how to thank God for His goodness to me—"

"Problem? Problem? What are you talking about, problem. You're going to have one good time here, kitten. Going to go mountain climbing, and swimming in the hot springs, now listen, your old Uncle Jim isn't going to let anything bad happen to you up here. You hear? You hear? No, sir. Nothing but happiness. Come on Betsy, don't let us down now, we're almost there. Can you see the lights yet?"

The camp was cupped in the bottom of a little valley. At first Marcella could make out only a scattering of lights, but then, as they drew closer, she saw the cabins themselves, rimming the edge of a ball field. Beyond the field, a couple of larger buildings stood—Jim pointed them out—a new chapel, built of logs like everything else, and the dining hall.

Jim stopped the car, grabbed Marcella's suitcase out of the back, and slipped a hand under her elbow to steer her down the dim path to a far cabin.

"Oh, what smells!" Marcella cried, overwhelmed by the scent of the surrounding pine forest.

"This is nothing," Jim replied. "This is still civilization. Wait until you get up there," he said pointing to a mountain.

"Are we going up top?" Marcella was having difficulty controlling the quaver in her voice. Too much was new: the mountains, the thin night air, the forest smells, the warmth of Big Jim's hand, the black shadow of him beside her.

"Sure are. Next Wednesday, my little sunflower. Old Yosemite Jim's going to round up all his chipmunks and make mountain goats out of them! We're going to backpack victuals, and sleeping gear—everybody lugs his own sleeping bag—and we'll stay all night long and come back Thursday."

"But Jim." Her thought stopped her. "I didn't know we were supposed to bring sleeping bags. I don't have one."

"Now don't you worry your pretty little head about it." His hand was under her elbow again, pacing her down the path beside him. "We'll just rustle up an extra one from somewhere. Maybe the cook has one, or one of the kitchen boys. Don't worry! You think this old goat is going to let you stay down here with the wart hogs while all his chipmunks are scampering up to the sky? Not on your life!

"Come on." His hand snapped out to pull open the cabin door. "Let's meet your cabin mates. They'll show you the ropes, help you hustle up a bite to eat, you must be hungry. That is," he poked his head through the inner door to a chorus of squeals and giggles, "if we can get them to stop talking long enough. You know, girls are pretty, generally speaking...and they're pretty generally speaking!"

15

Just being at camp made Marcella feel holy. Her eleven cabin mates were small town girls like herself, or farm girls, but they came from all over—Nebraska, Colorado, Arizona— some from towns she'd never heard of. Most of them were older, sixteen or seventeen, but—what blessing!—they considered themselves "children of God" every bit as much as she did. "What's your name" and "where are you from" were the first questions they asked, true, but "when were you saved" usually followed. So Marcella told them about the evangelical meeting, and about Big Jim (only of course not about their letters). She discovered that Big Jim had saved about half of the girls there, not just her (though she was the only one he wrote to, she felt certain). The rest had found God in summer revival tents, and some, like her bunk mate, Ronda, were such devout Christians that they'd been saved two or three times! Oh, what friends she could make here, she thought, but then she grew ashamed. How could she think of being close with anyone? Oh, she knew they were friendly, Ronda especially, but they must think that she was a good Christian, too. What if they *knew!* They were all so much better than she, how dare she even dream of being friends? She didn't know what to do, and then she remembered those books she'd read, about how doing "it" too much harms your outgoing personality, and she began to worry. Maybe that's what was making her so shy. Then she began thinking, maybe *that* was why God had saved her only once, because she wasn't good enough. She decided to ask Big Jim about it, first chance she got. In the meantime, she told herself, being here would be enough. So near Big Jim, and so close to God. So busy.

For they were busy. Mornings they studied the Bible, poring over the genealogies, the historical one and the other one, so they could refute anyone who claimed Jesus was not the Son of God, and learning how the four Gospels did not contradict one another, but fit all together, if you read them right. Afternoons they went to sports (mostly the boys played) or crafts. Marcella tried shooting arrows at a huge bull's eye, and liked that, and she made a billfold for her father by punching holes in pieces of leather and lacing them together. After supper, the campers met all together, to hold a song fest for the slides of the Holy Land, Galilee looking like Kansas, hills like bluffs, all arid and brown.

The girls in Marcella's cabin decided to start evening prayer meetings. Jane, their counselor, suggested it. They called themselves the "Goforths," after Jesus's admonition to go forth and preach the gospel. They met each night before lights out, reading from the Bible ("Where two or three are gathered together" became their favorite passage, almost like a motto), and sometimes singing. They talked a lot about what it meant to be a "Goforth," and what it meant to be "saved." Marcella hadn't known before how many times you could be saved, every day, really. She prayed that God would show Himself to her again, soon. Finally kneeling in a large circle and holding hands, the Goforths prayed, quietly and modestly at first—Marcella wished Jim could hear them—but then, led by some of the bolder Christians among them, chanting increasingly long, and increasingly impassioned, prayers, their ardent voices moaning into the silent mountain air.

"Wow, don't you girls ever lay off it?" some of the boys teased. But the Goforths paid no attention. "Speak of the Devil, and his horns appear," they said privately to one another. Besides, most of the boys didn't tease. Most were as pious as the girls.

As the days passed, Marcella kept trying to find a way to be alone with Jim, so they could talk. But it was difficult, he was so popular. Everywhere he went, kids clustered around him, listening to his jokes. When he wasn't surrounded, he was busy in his office, or out in the ball field, popping high flies to the boys. Marcella began to feel she wasn't so special, after all.

It was easier to find May, Jim's wife. She mostly stayed in their cabin, because of the baby, only five months old and as roly-poly as a Gerber's baby-food ad. Marcella hung around there several afternoons, hoping Jim would stop by, but he didn't, and talking to May just wasn't the same. She began to brood. Then one afternoon, while the baby was napping, May called the Goforths in, and talked of the danger of being concerned with things of the flesh. She told them women stories from the Bible, about Mary Magdalene, about Naomi and Ruth, about the two women, one who was faithful, and told them what a blessing it was for a woman to serve the Lord. Marcella felt pretty guilty, then. How could she let her mind dwell on so many petty things? She resolved not to think so much about talking to Jim, and to think more about serving God. She listened hard while May spoke to the Goforths about purity, and read them verses, like "Do not profane your daughter by making her a harlot, lest the land fall into harlotry and the land become full of wickedness."

The only ones at camp who didn't seem to be busy loving the Lord and learning about Him were the cook and the kitchen boys. They rattled and banged the pans around, even during before-meal prayers, and took the Lord's name in vain so often that Big Jim had to talk to them about it, so they didn't take His name in vain any more during meals (except they did it in Spanish, Ronda said), but sometimes, in the afternoon, if you happened to walk by the kitchen or go into the big dining hall to play Ping-Pong or shuffleboard, you could hear their swearing mingled with the clatter of the dishes.

The Goforths talked a lot about this. At first they thought maybe the Lord had sent the kitchen help to camp as a trial for the Christians. But then they decided, no, the Lord probably intended that the kitchen help be saved, that's why He'd brought them all the way from Mexico to work here. So the girls voted to go right into the kitchen and pray for them ("You do something evil if you do nothing good," they said, quoting Big Jim, she wished he could have heard them). But at the last minute, everybody was too chicken to start the prayers, so they just talked to the help about salvation. The cook, red-faced and sweating, snarled at them to get lost, while the kitchen boys giggled. The boys banded together and spoke rapid Spanish, then snapped their dish towels at the girls' backsides until the Goforths were forced to retreat. Lest they be thought harlots. Still, the girls kept right on praying for the lost souls of the boys, and even for the red-faced cook, praying night after night, in the tiny cabin.

16

The morning of the hike dawned warm and clear. Another of God's blessings. Marcella joined the campers clustered outside the dining hall—could camp already be almost over, Wednesday so soon, only a few more days to go? Would she ever get to talk to Jim?

"All right, who's gonna volunteer to climb first?" The line-up around Jim began. "First group totes sleeping gear, second group totes food. Here, Trump, you stay behind. We're gonna need your strong back later. Gotta have fleet of foot for this first group. There's more than one way to skin a cat, ah, not the same cat, of course."

Marcella wedged her way in. "Did you remember my sleeping bag?" she asked. Jim struck his head.

"Forget it! Didn't I forget all about it! Never mind. I'll speak to the cook myself, as soon as I get you chipmunks going. You go on ahead, I'll bring your bag with me. Old lard head himself...Sam? Where'd Sam go. Oh, there, Sam, round up some canvas straps out of my cabin, will you? Ask May for them."

The first group pulled out at 7 A.M.

"Don't forget to rest," Big Jim hollered at the disappearing hikers, loaded with sleeping bags and tarps, canteens swinging at the hips. "Don't try to make it all the way to the top in one spell, or we'll have to carry you down on stretchers."

Hiking was easy. The trail was marked well, crossing meadowy slopes before it came to anything the least bit mountainy. Then it skirted the rockiest terrain, wandering through the edge of a pine forest, before it headed up, up, up—across enormous deposits of glacial rock. Marcella's spirits lifted as they climbed. What a world this was, up here.

At first, the hikers stayed tightly together, singing "the bear went over the mountain," and kicking pebbles down the mountainside. Then the counselors split up, Sam taking the lead, brandishing his climbing stick, and Jane waiting to be last, so no one could accidentally get left behind. She carried the first-aid kit. As the trail narrowed, the hikers began to string farther and farther apart, each finding his own pace. By midmorning, Marcella was hiking alone.

That frightened her. What if something terrible should happen? What if she should slip? Fall? She was the youngest person climbing, not yet sixteen, not until September. What if she wore out? Or got lost? But then, stopping for a minute, she could still hear voices ahead of her. She could see blue trail markers everywhere, and she knew Jane was coming up behind. Gradually, her fears evaporated.

She breathed the thin mountain air more easily. How exhilarating it all was—even alone. More and more she looked around her as she walked, *On – ly God can make a blos – som, On – ly God can make a tree…*songs welling up, bursting inside her. She let her voice go, and heard her words echo back off the mountainsides. Oh! Kneeling, in gratitude, she saw still other things—wine and plum colors hiding the gray rocks, strange lichens as intricate as snow flakes. Was there no end to God's benevolence?

It was nearly nightfall by the time both groups reached the campsite on the edge of a large, nearly circular lake. Pine and rock stretched out endlessly.

Supper appetites were enormous. Marcella, like the other hikers, stacked her plate high with steaming food, returned for seconds, then thirds. "The noblest of all dogs, the hot dog. It feeds the hand that bites it," joked Jim. He left to tuck his two little boys in, then returned.

Once the sun set, the night air turned chilly. The blazing fire acted like a magnet, drawing the campers. They sang a song or two around it, limply harmonizing, laughing at the way the mountain spaces swallowed their voices. Then one by one, drooping with weariness, they left the fire and turned in.

Marcella, glad for the jacket over her flannel shirt, glad for her heavy underwear, waited while Jim raked out the embers. The cook, he explained, didn't have a sleeping bag after all, and the kitchen boys had already loaned theirs out, but it didn't matter. He'd double up his boys, and let her use one of theirs. How good of him, she felt, watching over her this way. They walked, crossing the deep black clearing behind the campfire, Jim's big lantern playing through the dark, to the sheltered area where his towheaded boys already slept.

"Shucks," Jim said. "This isn't going to work. Look how small their bags are. You couldn't fit into one of them." Marcella looked. He was right. She'd stick head and shoulders out, certainly. She watched, while Jim sat down and began unlacing his hiking boots, pulling them off, one by one.

"Here," Jim said. "You can just scramble in my bag alongside me. We'll have to double up, that's all."

It seemed a strange thing to do. Still, there wasn't much choice.

"Come on, pumpkin, don't just stand there," he said. "You can't very well sleep with your shoes on."

Marcella sat and obediently pulled them off.

"No, better leave that jacket on, princess. It's going to get mighty cold before sunup." Jim leaned over to unzip his sleeping bag. "Here," holding it open.

Marcella had a last-minute twinge of uncertainty, it seemed so strange to be *sleeping* with him. They had barely talked since the ride in from town, and now she was about to get into bed with him, well, not bed, exactly, but still…Of course, she needn't worry, after all, Jim was a man of God, almost like a minister, and what else was there to do? She'd freeze, trying to sleep in a child's short bag, and she couldn't very well bed down on the rocks, or ask Jim to. She said a brief silent prayer, and crept in.

Jim got in, too.

They both stretched out, and pushed their stockinged feet as far as they'd go. His toes were miles beyond hers. They laughed. That made her feel better. She watched while he sat up to zip the bag tightly around them. "This bag wasn't exactly built for two, you know," he commented. Then they both lay down, sliding partway under the top cover to keep their heads warm. Marcella pillowed her head against his arm. The air cooled her cheek. Stars glowed overhead. God seemed very close. She yawned.

"There they are," he said, "strung out all over the heavens. No rain tonight. Where's the Bear, the Big Bear? Spotted him yet?"

"I don't know that one," Marcella said, his rough sleeve prickling her cheek. Maybe she should talk to him now?

"Come on, pumpkin. Don't tell me none of those boyfriends of yours ever spotted the Big Dipper for you. Everybody knows that one."

Marcella blushed about the boyfriends, she wished he wasn't such a tease, that felt too much like her father, but she said only, "Is the Big Dipper the same as the Bear?"

"Sure. Just another name for him. Speaking of bears, know why the polar bear wears a fur coat?"

"No."

"Because he looks so silly in a cloth one....What are you giggling about? And look, over there, the Milky Way. Did any of those boyfriends of yours teach you how to spot the North Star?"

"I don't have any boyfriends. You know that."

"That's what they all say. Well?"

"Down the handle?" Her eyes kept getting heavy. Maybe they could talk in the morning.

"The tail, you mean?"

"Ummmmmmmm," Marcella said, no longer really listening, stars swimming in and out of her vision as her eyes blinked longer and longer shut.

"And then what do you do?"

Jim was sort of laughing, and half shaking, half squeezing her.

"What?" she said, waking suddenly. He laughed. "Bet you can't even tell Orion's belt from his sword."

"Mmmmmmmmmm," she began to drowse again. After a while he said, "What do you talk about with all those boys, anyway?"

But there was no answer, no answer at all.

She did not understand, later, much later, when she felt him pulling her. At first she thought it was morning already, and time to get up, but when she started to rouse herself, she heard Jim's voice whispering, "Shhhhh. Don't wake up, little sweetcake. Everything's okay."

Marcella opened her eyes. It was still black out. Her face was cuddled in his arm, and he seemed to be squeezing, or rocking her. She couldn't tell. "Shhhhh. Shhhhh. Go to sleep," his voice was like a lullaby, and he rocked her body back and forth. She slipped back into her sleep as quickly as she'd slipped out of it. But, and it seemed only an instant later, she was awakened again by the sound of his body, stirring, twisting, in the sleeping bag.

He was moving. His arm. Oh, his arm. "Here, princess, here. My arm's asleep, that's all."

Marcella slipped off his arm, plumping her head down on the place, flat, where his arm had been, still warm from his body heat, her eyes closing again, visions of, warm, red, nothing, only splotches of color, swimming. "No, no, that's no good. You'll get a stiff neck sleeping that way. Here. Use my chest as a pillow." But his chest was too high, mounding way up from the ground. "It's okay," she mumbled, trying desperately to hold on to the last fragment of her dream, the reds fading into yellow. Blinking.

"Here. Lay on top of me awhile." She felt his arms around her, lifting her, before she had time to think about it, drugged with sleep, his arms, around her, her body stretching out along his, her toes dropping down toward the ground in the space between his long legs, her cheek on his chest. He was stroking, stroking, her hair. "There, my little lollipop, better, huh? Back to sleep, kitten."

Jim made a strange mattress, firm and warm. At first she couldn't sleep. She kept feeling as it she were going to tumble right off him, as though she were a little girl afraid of falling out of a strange bed, but he put his arms around her, holding her secure, and began rocking, back and forth, every so gently. "Go to sleep, my pretty, go to sleep, my sweet."

The cold night air had rushed in as soon as they moved around, but already it was warm again. The sound of his lullaby voice, half talking, half singing, pulled her back into sleep, the visions swimming into view again, and out, then lingering, as she, dropping, floating, it was like lying on the bottom of a rowboat and feeling the river drifting underneath you

She had no idea whether she'd slept a little, or a long while, when the movements of his big body under hers started, like the rumbling of the earth. What's the matter? was her first thought, in near alarm, and then, oh, just Jim, stirring, probably can't sleep, maybe too heavy on him, maybe get down now, and she began to move. But there was…something. The way his hands, the way he had his hands on the small of her back, pressing, pressing down on her, there, in the small of her back, rubbing. He wasn't rocking anymore, it wasn't back and forth that he was moving, but in the opposite direction, the way the rope of a whip moves when you snap it, and his hands, weren't gentle, but pushing, pushing, against her, hard, in the small of her back, and hot. They seemed so hot, right down through her blue jeans, pressing on her, and she was scared, oh, frightened, what was he doing? Why couldn't she move? Roll off him

but there was something, about the way his body felt, no longer rippling like it had before, but hard, and tense, and stirring around, only stirring slightly now, like his legs were jumping, like he had the twitches, maybe even sleeping? maybe dreaming? Maybe he was having a nightmare, maybe that's what it was, and his body, stirring under hers, like sometimes when a dog sleeps, you can see how he's chasing rabbits, dreaming, and twitching in his sleep. But she knew it wasn't that, even as she calmed herself with the thought, she knew it wasn't dreaming but something else after all, something altogether else, though she had no name for it, and couldn't tell what it was.

She thought that she should go back to sleep, then, but her body, as she relaxed it, seemed to make his dream worse, for he began jerking, no! not a dream, really jerking! in the sleeping bag, but holding her, so tightly, holding her tightly against him, she must be wrong, he must be dreaming, having an awful nightmare, so stiffened, so stiffened had his body become, oh, terrible, and then he was moaning, moaning out loud in his sleep, a horrible sound, so that she couldn't begin to rest. "Jim," she whispered.

Then "Brother Morgan." She felt his body slacken, his body go all limp beneath her, and he was panting. Like she sometimes panted, but she pushed that thought hard away from her. "Are you all right?"

"Shhhhhhh," Jim said, breathing out so heavily that his breath almost became another moan. "Shhhhhh. It's nothing, nothing at all, little chickadee." He pulled her head down against his shoulders, and began rubbing her back with the small of his large hand, sing-songing, now, "Shhhhhhh. Shhhhhhh. Nothing at all. Nothing. Go to sleep, back to sleep, back to sleep, my baby." And his body, now that he was talking to her, was all relaxed, like before. She wondered if maybe she'd been dreaming. She closed her eyes, and waited for a while, until, the yellow, first, and then the red, splotches, swam out of her blackness to break against her eyes, before she let go, and drifted slowly, "shhhhhhhh, my baby," back to sleep.

❧ 17 ❧

When Marcella woke, Jim had vanished—down making the campfire, probably. At first, she felt relief, then she wished he had stayed…to talk to, to ask. Had she been dreaming? Or had he…? No. He couldn't have. Of course not. But…

The more she thought about it, the stranger it seemed. She didn't know what to make of it, she…still half asleep when he…she hardly remembered, had he…oh! Impossible! A minister of God would never…it must have been her own mind, playing tricks on her.

Jim greeted her at breakfast as though nothing was unusual. Marcella felt really funny then. How could she have supposed he, such a good Christian, could have been…certainly she had been dreaming.

It took them most of the day to hike down.

The last few days of camp sped by, filled with activities, including a trip to swim in the hot springs (the water was really warm, so blissful!) and the dedication of the new chapel. Then—could it be?—camp was almost over. It was the last evening, the last night of the last day…but she hadn't even talked to Jim yet! And tomorrow morning everyone would pack up their gear and get into cars, or buses, and go back to their Hildreths. It made Marcella's eyes mist to think about it.

After supper that night, everybody gathered in the chapel for the final service. Jim, in his white robe (it was the first time he'd worn it) joked around a bit, and then talked a long time about how we are all God's children and we mustn't think of how far away from each other we are all going, but only of how close together we all are, since we're all connected in God. Some of the kids cried.

The kitchen boys had a campfire blazing when chapel let out, and everybody roasted their last marshmallows, and sang "Waltzing Matilda" and a bunch of silly songs, and laughed a lot, so that it was already pretty late when Big Jim—back in his T-shirt and sneakers after the service—shooed everybody along to bed. Not that everyone went, of course. Some headed out for a last walk along the edge of the forest that bordered the camp. Marcella watched them go; it was like seeing couples sneak out early from MYF. Other kids headed down to the boys' cabin, a favorite hangout. Marcella dallied awhile, watching the kitchen boys stir and rake the embers down. One of them tried to talk to her in his broken English, but she felt uncomfortable, and moved away.

She started walking across the clearing of the ball field, farther and farther, until she had an almost unobstructed view of the mountain sky, pitch-black and even more vast than the interminable sky of the prairie. Each star stood out, distinct and separate, even in the Milky Way.

Marcella wished camp weren't over. It had been so good. She hadn't done it once, not even once, and none before two weeks before she came—by the time she got home again, it would be three weeks without…a new record. She had really wanted to talk with Jim, of course, she was so disappointed that she hadn't, and now it was too late. She was sad, too, that God hadn't saved her again, like He had Ronda, sad that she hadn't made a close friend.

She had been standing there long enough to begin thinking that she ought to return to her cabin, where the Goforths were probably already praying, when she saw a form coming across the field toward her, moving slowly. Finally she could make out that it was Big Jim, and she raised an arm in greeting.

"Halloooooo out there," he yodeled, making her laugh.

"Hallooooo," she yodeled back, waiting until he got closer before saying, "Hi, Jim." She was happy to see him, but nervous a bit too. Maybe they could talk now?

"Knock, knock," he said, his stride closing the distance between them.

"Who's there."

"Little old lady."

Marcella knew what was coming, but played along.

"Little old lady who?"

"Aha," he cried, pointing his finger, "I didn't know you could yodel! What are you doing way out here on a night like tonight? All we need's a full moon, and everybody'd be baying from the bushes, eh chickadee?"

"Watching the stars," she replied, shyly, "just thinking about what you said tonight." How could she bring it up?

"Mmmmmm. D'ja ever find old Papa Bear?"

She pointed.

"And Baby Bear?"

She pointed again. "Over there."

"Very good, very good. Someone must be giving you lessons. Now tell me what has four legs and flies."

"A dead horse," she replied. She'd heard him tell that one this afternoon.

"Hey! Getting to be a wise guy, huh."

They stood and talked a while, about camp, and the Northern Lights. She kept trying to bring up "that," but each time she thought of something she might say, she turned mute with embarrassment. Finally Jim said, "Come on," and they headed back to the campfire. She would never get to talk to him now. She tried to keep her mind on what he was saying—some more about the stars—but he was walking so close to her, she found it hard to listen. She could feel his body warmth, its heat touching her, its strength, almost magnetic, so tangible that it upset her, but she couldn't seem to pull herself away.

"You know, princess, I love these stars up here. They seem so near, it looks like you could reach right up and touch them."

Was it her imagination, or were his clothes actually brushing her? She made no reply. He didn't speak again, either, and they walked in silence, watching the sky. A star fell.

"Oh! Did you see that?" She turned to look up at him.

"Mmmmmm, hmmmmm," he said, stopping too, but he wasn't looking at the sky. They were so close! She could feel his breath unexpectedly soft against her forehead. It made her a bit queasy, though what could be wrong, them standing there, watching the stars together. But just the same, he was so close. She was beginning to think that maybe she should move away from him a little, maybe she should speak or something, when he moved—away—then broke entirely, turning to say, "Wait a minute," before he headed past the campfire into the dining hall. What a funny thing to do. Maybe he forgot to tell the cook something, and wanted to leave him a message.

Marcella shrugged her shoulders, and waited. She felt calmer, now that he had gone. She looked at the stars again, and at the dead coals where the fire had been. A shiver raised goose pimples along her arm. She should go back to her cabin: if she didn't return pretty soon, the Goforths would be finished with prayers, and everybody would be in bed. Just the same, she waited. When Jim still didn't return, she thought maybe she'd better find him and tell him that she was going to turn in.

The dining hall was pitch-dark. It took a few moments for her eyes to adjust to this new black, no longer starlit. She saw the room was bare, empty as a barn, its wooden tables stacked against the wall. The echoings of Ping-Pong balls, the rumblings of mealtimes, the scrapings of chairs: all were stilled.

"Jim?" she called, uncertainly. There was no answer. How queer. "Jim?" she called, louder. Where had he gone? Then she heard his voice—stifled—edging into the dining room from the kitchen. "I'm in here. Just a minute." She waited. She could feel her hairs prickling. When she heard his voice again it was closer, but it had a hard and unfamiliar edge.

"What made you come in here?" he asked. Marcella suddenly felt the edge of her fear—and something else—rising. Then she saw him moving like a dark silhouette. She became giddy.

"I don't know," she replied, giggling, forgetting what she'd come to say. "I wanted to know where you were."

"I'm here," he said, stopping halfway across the room. His shadowy form tugged at her like gravity, like his body heat had before, when they were walking. What was he doing? What did he mean, "I'm here"? She felt another giggle starting, but her fear stifled it. She wanted to run, but she couldn't. Standing still was the only resistance she could muster to…whatever was pulling her…

"Well," he said, in a gravelly voice, "come here, then," and he stretched his arm out to her.

Oh, she could not go, she dared not, impossible…but she was going, moving, slowly drawn across the great space to him, dear God, forgive. Her face, the muscles in her face, kept tightening, until her whole face felt like river-bottom mud in the summer, all dry and close to cracking…what did he want of her? what was this pulling?

She put out her small hand to meet his, thinking that maybe they would stand together, as they had before, maybe they would hold hands, even, because it was the last night. But when their hands met, he seized her, and kissed her.

It happened so swiftly. The harshness of his skin, his arms, so tough, there seemed no gentleness in him, his belt buckle scraping against her, his warmth, that hotness seeping out of his very flesh. And there was his incredible size, the enormity of him, her body so diminished by his, she felt as stiff and slender as an arrow. He began lifting her, pulling her up, up, up along him, pulling her high up on him, and then she felt him: she felt it, and she knew, now, what it was there, beneath his summer trousers, or maybe even out of them, she could feel it, stiffened, right there, and then, no! thrusting, and thrusting, oh! right against her, pushing, insisting, *right there,* he was pushing it, *right there,* only her pants prevented...and she had written him, Oh, Jim, it is harder if I date, in that...oh! back and forth he was pushing it, there was no mistaking it, it was not a dream, it was as real as the living-room pillow, making that electric tingling run up and down her spine, oh JIM! Harder and harder. She fought it. She fought her understanding, and she fought the ugly pictures forming in her mind, she fought it all—the incredible knowledge of oh JIM Oh! *him,* Bro – ther Mor – gan, and the (disgusting) recognition of her own (tingling) body, yielding, yielding, it was yielding to him, to his

Her whole body stiffened. This was no longer unfamiliar. It was all too familiar, that interminable old battle, shifted to a new plane, no longer private...She squirmed, and wanted to cry out, but didn't. She struggled—and not just against herself, but against the only person who (I don't know how to thank God for His goodness to me) *oh!* She wanted to yell, but dared not. She needed all of her breath to help her with the furious pummeling, pummeling, pummeling of her fists.

She was stunned when she broke his hold, and nearly fell before she could right herself and begin running. Behind her was silence, then footsteps, and then his voice, calling, "Marcella!" But, determined, she ran on. She was having none of that.

❧ 18 ☙

Marcella thought her bus would never come. She'd made a point of leaving with the early group, scrambling into the camp station wagon, spinning down the dirt road, girls squealing at every bounce, pine trees whirling by. Most of the kids left on the Denver Trailways, but she had to wait for the Greyhound. Three hours, just to make her connection.

The station was cramped and dirty. There was nothing to do. She drank a Coke at the soda fountain and looked over the magazines. They were mostly movie magazines, things of the flesh and not worth reading. She sat huddled in a corner, waiting, and watching the road. When Jim's car pulled in with a later group, she fled to the restroom, locking herself in a stall. She didn't come out until it was nearly time for her bus.

Jim wasn't there. She bought a ham sandwich and a bag of potato chips to take on board.

The Greyhound driver pulled out of the little mountain town, then barreled down the road, tires squealing on hairpin turns until Marcella felt sick. She tried to open her window, but it was stuck. The inside of her head kept swelling, getting tighter and tighter until *pop!* her ears released the pressure. She searched her purse for chewing gum, but found none, so she tried swallowing, instead. The dour man beside her kept popping Chiclets into his mouth. "It helps if you chew gum," he said, but he didn't offer her any and she was too timid to ask. So she clutched her purse, and kept swallowing, praying God not to let her throw up at least until the bus stopped. She rode down out of the mountains that way.

At Denver, they stopped long enough for her to get out and buy a Coke and some Dentyne. The man with chewing gum got off, and a sheepherder from Montana sat beside her. He winked, and talked, then suddenly slept, jaw dropping wide open. "Don't listen to him," a fat woman in a print dress behind Marcella kept leaning forward and insisting. "He's drunk." When they got off, the ride was better.

Marcella ate her sandwich and chewed some gum, even though her ears had stopped popping. She wished she'd thought to buy something to read; she knew most of the Burma Shave signs by heart now. She tried to read her Bible; it was no good. The white Testament only made her think of him. Once she thought she heard a noon whistle blowing, but it had to be later than 12 o'clock. She never looked back to see the mountains disappear.

The bus kept pushing on down the road, in and out of little towns, stopping at filling stations and crossroads. And in between, only telephone poles, as stark against the sky as crosses. Marcella tried to sleep, but it was no good, so she sat staring, trying not to think, watching tumbleweeds rattle across pastures. "I am like Jerusalem," she thought, remembering the verses memorized from Lamentations: *She weepeth sore in the night, and her tears are on her cheeks: all her friends have dealt treacherously with her, they are become her enemies.*

She began putting it all together, then, understanding—the diagrams in that book her mother had given her, and what they meant. At least her pants were on; at least he hadn't been able to come in, oh! and she understood what her fingers were the substitute for, and why it was like peeping through a keyhole on marriage. How could he do it, with May right down there in their cabin? How could…oh, and she understood why kissing made it so much harder; how she wished she'd never written that to him! She, who wouldn't even sit on the front porch swing beside her father, what would her father think now? How could she have been so blind, so stupid, she was no better than Rosemary in the piney woods, oh, every bit as bad as Rosemary, who had let a man feel her…and now she understood what that meant, that is exactly what she, Marcella, had done…let a man, yes, oh, please forgive, and let him not once, but twice, oh, dear God, and she had known! Really, she had known, hadn't she, at least with a small part of her being, she had known, then, walking toward him in the dining hall. Maybe she had even known before.

Harlot.

The air got hotter and hotter inside the bus. She struggled to open the window, but still it would not give. Outside, dust whirled across the road from the plowed fields. The driver had to use his wipers to clear the silt off the windshield. Overhead, the sky remained motionless and blue, that flat pale blue of a late summer prairie sky, giving nothing, retaining nothing, barely stretching wide enough to cover the fields below. The long corn leaves, dry and brown, rattled and cracked in the wind, she knew, even though there in the bus she heard nothing but the drone of the tires on the asphalt. She wondered if it had been this bad in Galilee. She didn't think so. The Bible was filled with stories about fishermen, they must have had water; there was no water here, none, not in the summer, anyway, little creeks stone dry, mud cracking, turning up into the sun, curling, the mud pulled as tight as, her face, had been when she walked toward him, holding out her hand…oh. Why couldn't she cry? Turgid with tears, but her eyes as dry as parched prairie bones. She knew why. She had profaned…not just herself, but herself and him, a minister of God Almighty, even the land was falling into wickedness, as May had read it would. All this dust, it was a sign. God would never forgive her.

❧ 19 ❧

One, two, buckle your shoe, I know what I'd like to do STOP!

Our Father who art in Heaven, hallowed be Thy name. Thy kingdom come come come come STOP!

Thy kingdom come, thy will be done, that's better. That's better. *On earth as it is in heaven.* See. It's really not that hard, hard, hard, STOP!

One, two buckle your NO! just a girl who can't say NO! NO! STOP STOP STOP STOP

Oh, dear God, oh dear God in Heaven, please help me. I don't want to, really I don't, I mean maybe I wanted to a little bit before and that is why I gave in to temptation, I know I said that I didn't want to before, but this time I really mean it! Oh dear Lord, there must be some place, some place I can go where

Marcella's fingers slid down over her belly, down, down, down, across the danger zone below her bellybutton, marching, closer, closer. The night breeze blew across her bare legs. Crickets sang. She began rocking back and forth. Back and forth

before I

before I

The words were like a crooning

before I *do*

before I *do*

Coaxing her, leading her, half asleep. Her fingers slipped lower and lower.

before I *do* it.

Before I do it! *Oh, no!* The words jolted her out of her drifting, jolted her eyes wide open. She jerked her fingers OFF, looking at her hand as though it were some strange foreign thing, placed on the end of her arm to torture her. *Oh, NO! Not again!* Her head in her hands, she sat, rocking, but this time in despair. No! No! No!

It was inconceivable, how difficult...thirty-five days since she had...longer than she'd ever gone before, longer even than when she first found out she was...doing it, oh, she'd stopped for several weeks then, but never ever for a whole *month* before, but how difficult! No one to talk to, no one to write to. But how could God forgive her if she didn't actually stop? But how incredibly badly she'd been wanting, to do it, and it coming upon her like this, it was too hard...

She pushed herself out of bed, and pulled her jeans over her pink summer nightie pants, tucking the pajama top in like an undershirt. Sweater, where is a sweater. Or a shirt, where did I put it...still summer by day, but already autumn chilled the night air. She knew. She'd been walking a lot, last night, and the night before, and. So afraid her mother would find out, or even worse, her father—sneaking out to meet someone, he'd say. But still, this risk, less than the other.

Tomorrow, surely, if tomorrow I can hold out, then the weekend. That's not bad, so much more to do. Oh, if only I can, then school will start, and organ lessons. So much to do, then, and boy, would she keep busy! Just you wait and see, God. I'll try out for chorus, and band, and maybe work on the yearbook, and teach Sunday school, and volunteer at MYF, and practice the piano and the organ every day, and then, oh, then, certainly it will get easier.

If she were right. If it really were a habit you could break, like drinking, or smoking, lots of people gave those habits up, and it was hard at first, oh, she'd read in *Reader's Digest* what an alcoholic had to say, and she didn't think it would be easy, but if she were right, in a month, or two months, or three, oh, if she could only hold out, then it would be GONE!

And if she couldn't?

If she were wrong?

Marcella began to cry, bending over her dresser, leaning her head deep into the cradle of her arms, crying, leaning her forehead against the varnished wood. The smell! Oh, NO, the same smell! The very same smell as when she used to…finish, the smell, of varnished wood, and her fingers, sore, sore, from the pushing, the pushing and the holding, holding, of the fingers, in so very deep, oh, and hard, and wiggling only the very tips of them, hard, back down against the

Oh, NO! Her mind, kept running like this, and worse, and always, her hand creeping down in the middle, like now, and I've got to get out of here

She had to slow down in case her parents were awake. She turned the doorknob, a fraction of an inch at a time, like the minute hand on a clock, moving. Lifting the door as she pushed, so the hinges wouldn't creak. She knew all the tricks—soft, along the edges of the hallway, close to the baseboard so the floor won't sound, tiptoe, and down the stairs, quiet, quiet, one step at a time, feet along the outside of the steps, soft, soft, the landing, careful, but then the carpet, oh, the blessed carpet!

The streetlight dropped a white cone in the darkness. She paused, wondering which way to go. So quiet out, like death.

No sound, no human sound anyway, only crickets, and maybe frogs…She set off to the east, what's that? A noise…she backtracked quickly.

You had to watch it. She'd worn shoes the first night, but they made so much racket she took them off. Now she came out barefoot, even though that made running harder…she'd have to be careful.

Crossing streets was the worst. It put you right out into the open where—what was that? She froze an instant, listening, but heard nothing else, so she went on, moving closer to the hedges—for protection. Crossing streets, anybody could see you. You'd be right out in the open, no place to duck, and he'd probably say, "Oh, she's just asking for it," and crying no good because how could the neighbors hear? how could they hear with his hand muffling her screams, them probably asleep anyway

There it was. Again. She was right the first time. A sound. Like? Someone walking? Too? On the grass, like she was, walking, soft as soft, hiding his footsteps in the tender grass, oh, she could hear him really well now, oh! over by the bushes, there, she could even see him moving, the branches parting, there, oh, dear God in Heaven, please protect me, oh, I know I don't deserve it, but please look down and

A cat.

It really was a cat, strolling out from behind the hedge, then freezing at her sound, its head turning, eyes mirrored in the dark, no!

It fled.

She didn't know whether to laugh or to cry. At least she was alive for one more day, whether that was good or not

She went home the back way, picking her path down the alley cautiously, circling the house to get in at the front door. As soon as she got to her room and climbed in bed, it began again.

There was nothing to do but write. She wrote everything in her diary, now, but carefully, in case Lucille should read it... oh, if anyone knew what a heinous sin she had committed, and maybe it was like a virus, maybe someone could catch the awful habit reading what she'd written, like when she'd read about women masturbators.

"Oh my God," she wrote, "how to stop this awful craving! What to do. What to do. I want it, how I want it, my whole being wants it." She was careful not to write "body," in case someone might guess.

"Sometimes I am strong enough. Sometimes. Always, so far. But I doubt my strength. Can I really win? Oh, but I must. I must. If I don't, what kind of punishment will that bring? There is no choice. It's either it, or me. I have to win.

"Oh, but oh, what is there to do? What? And when will it ever end. When, when, when, when"

She stopped, and flipped to the back pages where she kept a chart. She wrote yesterday's date, and checked off:

    x   yes, I thought about it

    x   yes, I came close (her coding for touching)

And, proudly, the x that really counted:

    x   no, I did not do it.

Touching didn't count. It was a sin, of course, and eventually she would have to stop, but right now, when the struggle was so gigantic, right now she won if she didn't stick, anything, *in,* if she didn't actually make spasms come. For thirty-five...thirty-six, now...days, she had not.

Some days she could check off the "no, I didn't come close" space. Those were very good days. But not once had she been able to check that she had not thought about it.

Some days it seemed as though she could think of little else.

Oh, but it was more important than ever before! Because of what she knew, of course, because of Big Jim—not that she was writing him any more. She'd burned all his letters as soon as she'd got back, all of them, his address, too, and hidden the New Testament, which she didn't dare burn. And resolved not to answer his letters—"I'll show him! I'll tear it up before I even open it"—but no letter came. After a while, she stopped looking for one.

If only she could hold out, a little longer, then…surely, goodness and mercy, her body would revert, back to…like it was before, in the bathtub, with her hair just beginning to show, so exciting, growing up, and no problems then. Oh, if she had known what was ahead of her, what she was destined to do, oh, if she had known the depth of the perversion, the sin, then, surely, God's will be done, she never would have started. And if she hadn't begun, she never would have gotten into this habit. Filthy, perverted habit.

She would *not* give in, no, she would not. Oh, now she knew how hard to was to be a perfect Christian, all right. She used to think it would be easy, that it really was only a matter of determination, but now, she knew how difficult it was, how few could ever make it. The sort of temptation God put her through… as though the masturbating thing was a test, hideous but real, like Jesus and his forty days in the desert. God was sending her through the Valley of the Temptation to see if she was worthy of His blessed forgiveness, and Satan was tugging at her daily, oh, she'd never *dreamt* it would be so difficult…but she was going to make it. Somehow, she would reach the other side. She would be a Christian, a real Christian, all the way. No, she would not let herself be thrown off the track by sin. No, not. She had made up her mind.

Finally, she slept.

Everywhere was black. Black above her, black around her, black even below her. She was like her own ghost, walking on nothing, like you do in dreams, and everywhere black. But she was there—she could feel herself moving, moving, forward in time, and happy, but also a little unhappy, as though she were out taking one of those walks of her, oh, maybe even a daylight walk clear out of town by the riverbanks, and happy, watching the redwing blackbirds, and the orioles, fly, and breaking the cracked riverbed mud curls, but also unhappy, because of why walking here, what escaping. It was like that.

Nobody else was there, only her, alone, moving, and it was getting lighter. Then there they were, three white shapes. At first she thought they were men, but then they were so white, and so much light all around them that she knew they were God's angels—the way it is, when you're asleep, and you know you're dreaming, but you don't wake up.

They've come to walk with me.

Floating, more than walking, nearer, and nearer.

Then too near. They were getting too near, their heavy faces more gray than white, and her happiness fading like the black was fading, they were getting so close, too close, saying nothing, nothing, but she knew that they were going to get her, oh, and she should run away, but she couldn't, she couldn't move her arms and legs, there was something wrong with them, they were like wet bread dough and she couldn't move them, oh! No more black left, only gray, and faces, and her limbs. They pinned her! They pinned her down! Their faces, smiling, and behind their faces, their arms, moving, moving UP and down and UP and down and UP and

She felt it. She couldn't see it, but she felt it, it felt like water, warm water, they were pouring warm water—down there!—but as soon as she thought it, they were grinning, oh, and their teeth as gray as their faces, and grinning, and it wasn't water, warm, but no, it was oh my God, too solid for water, and it was oh it was HUGE, she could see it, on the horizon, HUGE and red, swirling around, and around, and

DOWN and up and DOWN and DOWN and down again UP down down down down

screaming

They were inside her. They were putting that *thing* inside her, they had it clear UP her, she could FEEL it, it was warm, and running out between her legs like *water* and

screaming

FINGERS up there, INSIDE OF HER, oh NO! My God, dear God, please *forgive* me, how had they gotten up there, her fingers, that's what was all the time UP INSIDE of her, what she'd been feeling and

out of bed. Oh! Oh! Running down the hall, I don't care if she *does* hear me, into the bathroom, already morning, the sun streaming through the window, oh help me somebody, and to the sink. where. yes. water. cold. oh, *cold* water give me, and splashing it all over her face, where was her mother? why wasn't she calling up the stairs, "Marcella, is that you? Making all that noise?" why wasn't she coming?

dreaming. that's all, only dreaming, couldn't possibly get your fingers up there in your sleep, how could you? But it was no use pretending. Her fingers were still sticky, white goo all over them, yes, there, still, now, sticky

Soap! Water! Hot, water, ow! oh I don't care if it's scalding me, I should burn them OFF, I should throw them AWAY, did not Jesus Himself say: *And if thy right eye offend thee, pluck it out, and cast it from thee: for it is profitable for thee that one of thy members should perish, and not that thy whole body should be cast into hell. And if thy right hand offend thee, cut it off and cast it from thee:* cut it off and cut it off and, cut it off off off OFF

Oh holy mary mother of god pray for me now and in the hour of my sin

WHERE IS MY MOTHER? WHY ISN'T SHE CALLING, "MARCELLA, IS IT YOU, CRYING?"

Cut it OFF and

picking up the razor and

picking up the razor and

yes, picking up the razor that, oh, yes, the extra razor that, her father, yes, wanted to throw away, when he got his new one, but her mother said keep, yes, you can use it when you're traveling, and

cut it OFF and

yes, the razor and, yes, the razor and, yes, better to cut it OFF than be cast into the everlasting fire and, opening

it up

opening the razor

UP

the razor BLADE double-edged blade oh you might as well keep it, her mother said, you're always losing razors, never know when you might need it, or even company, someone else might want to, yes, better to pluck it out than risk

yes

and her hands, trembling, as she fumbled with the opening, her hands, trembling, knocked the blade down into the sink, and picking it up, oh, not too carefully, the fingers, sliced, a little, bleeding, oh, the red blood, of Marcella, better to, oh, the blood

MY GOD, MY GOD, WHY HAST THOU

You can't cut off your fingers with a razor blade, stupid. Blades can't cut through bone.

oh, yes, better to cut if OFF than

But even Mrs. Schneider has to use a hatchet to cut her chicken's head off, how can you cut a finger off with just a blade? And the pain, the pain of all the flesh cut when the razor goes through, and tries to cut the bone, but only ripping all the flesh up, and then what will you tell people…

So she began sucking her cut fingers, instead, and whimpering, and wondering where was her mother. Her mother was her only salvation on really bad days, Marcella could follow her around the house, from room to room, where was she, and why wasn't she here, and why had nobody HEARD

Marcella put Band-Aids on her hurt fingers. Two fingers. Barely cut. On her left hand. Then she dressed. The heat was already heavy in her room. She pulled her shades against the afternoon sun. How still the house was. It seemed as though no one was home. But soon Mr. Colby would be. She could have lunch with him and maybe go downtown for a while. Even if her mother was gone, outdoors maybe, in the yard, and even if Lucille…

She went downstairs. The rooms were dim, Venetian blinds drawn. She called, but there was no answer. She called outdoors. Quiet. The note was in the kitchen:

"Marcella, I had to go over to Sadie's. John took a turn for the worse last night, and she needs help. Lucille went out biking with friends. Your father has Rotary today, won't be home for lunch.

Don't mess up the kitchen. Mother."

Alone. Oh, no, not alone. Not today. Not after last night, this morning. She reached into the cupboard and pulled out the Raisin Bran. Always, somebody around, she needed somebody, anybody, even Lucille better than being alone. She poured milk over the cereal, and watched while the autumn leaves of bran soaked it up. And couldn't go over to Sadie's, that was grown-up stuff. Mrs. Colby would be mad if she broke into it for "no reason at all."

Marcella took a bite. It needed sugar. She didn't feel like getting up for it. She took another bite. It stuck in her throat. She felt tears behind her eyes; it was no use. She couldn't possibly keep on holding out, it was too much for her. Like a pattern. She knew that now. And nowhere to go to escape it... she tried hard to swallow.

can't even eat in peace.

Marcella threw the rest of her cereal out, rinsed the bowl and stacked it in the drainer. Not safe, anywhere.

The living room was stuffy and dim, the heat already filtering in from outdoors. She switched the fan on. Its Mickey Mouse ears began to spin. Maybe if she practiced the piano.

The thick carpet hid the sound of her steps.

She pulled her Czerny out, and warmed up with good old C major, no sharps, no flats, just do, re, mi, fa, sol, la, ti, do, ti, la, sol, fa, mi, re...Up and down she went, up and down, the music weaving patterns in the air like threads of a huge tapestry. Her thoughts, weaving a pattern of their own behind the web of music, out, out, into the room. Even her...sin...had its pattern, its form: she'd known, from long before, when she first promised never, do, re, mi, never, ever, la, ti, to do it again. Trying to stop, that had a pattern, too, a rising up and falling off, like the waxing and the waning of God's own moon, oh, no, He wouldn't do that, how could He? It must be inside her. Or the Devil. But she knew it was there. She knew—how it ebbed, after her period was done, how it ebbed awhile, then rose, and rose, until, at the halfway point, when the moon, if it were the moon, would be barely half-full, then...the feelings, would begin, to crest, oh! and she would do it once, twice, maybe three times, at night, or in the morning, or in the afternoon, anytime, anytime at all, sitting, standing, walking, roaming around, it didn't matter, she would be half crazy for it. Like now. But her period was over! Done! The feelings, should be ebbing, not rising up, and up, and up, and up, Dear God, please make it crest soon...

If only she could ride it through. A few weeks until school, she'd be so busy then, if only it would, oh, say yes, God, ebb away.

Around her, the music flowed.

Oh, why hadn't someone stayed home?

She mustn't stop playing now, she mustn't, or her feelings would overflow, overwhelm her...her own fault, anyway, thinking so much about it, but it was so hard, putting it away from her mind, especially the good times, before she knew. How it would rise, slowly, and then sharply, as her breasts began to swell, and she would begin to think, oh, I am doing it *so much* again, *so often*, and then the curse would be there, and she would be flowing, flowing, and aching with the flow, oh, her desire at its highest then. Its apex. Her Kotex riding high in her crotch, rubbing hard against her groin, and wanting to! Oh, that was the hardest part to control, now, the wanting, how it descended upon her, the wanting, and having to say no, no, no, no. But then, before

Then she didn't have to.

Then she could, oh, anything—take her panties off, do it, naked, or in a skirt, yes, a wraparound, so good for hiding, she could cover herself up quickly, not like these jeans, having to zip them up and everything.

But even then, dreading it, a little, on "those" days. Because of the bloody fingers, of course, that was awful. "Oh," she would ask herself, "how can you do something like this?" Staring at her fingers, stained with red, or maybe only with a trace of it, around her fingernails, maybe she wouldn't see it right away, but later, examining a cuticle, there it would be: all brown and crusty, looking like a day-old Kotex. "Oh," she would say, "how awful." But she would do it anyway.

And bad, not just because of the bloody fingers, oh, God, forgive me, I didn't know what I did, I did not know, but also because of the terrible force of the desire. Wanting, oh how wanting! It hadn't seemed quite right, even then. She was always glad when it was over, the wave receding, so she could go about her business like her old self, before the breasts, and the hair, and one day, yes, sitting at the piano, do, re, mi, practicing, the Kotex, la, ti, pushing right into her, do re, every time she reached for the pedal, mi, wiggling, la, like now, her jeans, and sometimes catching. It made her ache so, to feel it, and not to touch herself. Of course she couldn't stop, or Mrs. Colby would say, "Your half-hour isn't up yet," so, dear God, she kept twisting, her body, when she played, like this, twisting, back and forth, so the Kotex rubbed, rubbed, rubbed, oh! against her, yes! and she got so worked up she had to stop, or else do it, right HERE, on the piano bench, with her mother, but she couldn't, oh dear God, please help me STOP THIS

Pretending. Pretending. "But I have to, mother, I have to go now. I can't wait. The pin is sticking me!" Oh, lying, and her mother, believing

How good it felt. Marcella, pulling, the elastic, up tight, walking upstairs, so s-l-o-w-l-y, legs held tight, and pulling, on the elastic, so it would rub, like those pillows, over there, on the davenport, rubbing all the way, up, the stairs, not even making it *into the bedroom!* Oh, but wanting it, so much—into the bathroom, dear God, forgive, hardly shutting the door, before, down, yes DOWN, on the FLOOR, down, oh, HARD, and fingers, way, in, up, around, aaaaaaaahhhhhhhh, and the spasms, starting, coming even before she could feel the cold, how very cold the tile, against the knuckles of her right hand, cold, cramped hand knuckles, cold, yes, against her cheek, cold, and the tiles, yes God, leaving, she saw them in the mirror, red marks. On her cheeks.

She tore her hands away from jeans where they had dropped… oh, no! She raised them up, staring at the Band-aids—only this morning, and

making two fists, slammed the keyboard with all her strength and screamed, "Oh, no! Why did they have to go? Today. No! No! No!"

Her voice echoed in the silent room. The fan whirled away. And everywhere she looked…something. The pillows. The davenport. The rug. Everywhere. The rug, stretching on and on, its rose-beige tufts so rough against her legs. No! Stop! Oh, yes, she'd done it there too

beckoning her. Like her bed, upstairs, always beckoning, enticing her to

how she'd burned her legs on the rug, re, mi, burned a big red burn all along her shin, fa, sol, she had burned it, rubbing, rubbing, rubbing, into the rug, and not caring, caring only for the spasms, *right then,* and the skin of her leg all red and raw they were not home that day, either, she had been practicing, and let herself down, and

OH, NO!

the fan, whirring away ti la sol fa and the rug and

maybe cold baths would do it. Maybe if she got up right away and took a cold bath, but no, she would have to take her clothes off, and it was always harder NOT to do it when she was naked, besides, over the rim of the bathtub, once, riding, on the horse of the bathtub rim, oh, good, and slipping, down into the water, and wanting MORE MORE MORE MORE, the water so warm, and pushing white soapy fingers in, and then HAVING to try it again, just once, she said, once more, over, her wet legs slipping on the edge, and her fingers, helping, but oh! and with the soap bar! and coming, and oh, and coming, and oh, and coming, and oh, she had to clean the mess up after, water, all over the floor, and she didn't even care, no, she did it there, too, with the warm washcloth, all wet and squishing, she only wanted to do it JUST THIS ONCE MORE GOD, AND THEN I'LL NEVER EVER EVER

Oh, no!

oh, yes, says Rastus, there we was on the railroad tracks, and the train was coming, and she was coming, and I was coming, it was one of Cheryl's awful jokes, and the train was the only one could STOP! STOP!

Filth, such filth, where did Cheryl learn those dirty jokes anyway, about the circus lady, who did it, with a pop bottle, oh, how disgusting! didja hear? stuck a bottle up there (old witch lives in a cave does it with corncobs) and pushed it up and down, and up and down, and then—oh, God, forgive me for remembering— it caught. Suction. Caught. Paid her to do it, it was part of her act. She pulled her whole insides out. Out! OUT! Hanging outside of her body, red and wet, and the kids all laughing, how did she get it off, Cheryl? How OFF? Bottle hanging, insides, red, guts, like chicken entrails, out, how OFF? OFF?

STOP she couldn't STOP IT water all over the floor, oh, coming, and the warm, the warm water, so good, oh, yes, there was nothing, she wouldn't try, when they were gone, from home, when she was all alone, oh, no

the lady smashed it. that broke the suction. smash. crackle. pop. no more insides hanging out. they snapped back. like a rubber band band band band band band band STOP

and the cold, the cold of the tub, she never knew how good cold could feel, and maybe she should, right now, go take an ice cube, just once, a little one, to remember how good it did feel, Oh, God, please forgive, yes, and carried it upstairs, on a washcloth, so she wouldn't drip water on the floor, and yes she had, dear God, she knew not, what, it would do re mi feel like, with an ICE cube

cold, skin pulling hard away. get another, yes another, on such a hot day as this, how about a good a tall a cold NO STOP how about a nice long tall bottle of soda pop NO NO would feel, or maybe BOTH, yes BOTH, first the ice, and then the bottle of pop, come on, Marcella, how about it, just once, the skin pulling away, hard, and the fingers, oh, cold, she would come a thousand times to the touch it had been so long, yes, so long Lord, then, before she knew what she was do re mi fa sol la ti doing and there was nowhere to GO

WHY DID THEY HAVE TO LEAVE TODAY?

where could she go, oh, no use trying to play any more, everything reminded her, no use practicing, alone, in the empty house, everything pulling, tugging, my jeans, the rug, the pillows on the davenport, COME inviting her COME

come, take, eat, this is my body given for

run! but her limbs, like wet dough

come. here. come to me. The rug. Dear God, the rug, the songs, I come, I come, *I come to the Gar – den a – lone,* they would not leave her, alone, and the rug, so rough its tufts underneath her toes, so rough and still come, come, come to me only NO!

She would only have to drop, down, on it, right here, yes, and unzip her jeans, yes, NO! her fingers began to fiddle with the snap button, her fingers, fiddling *come* her fingers starting their serenade, *come lovely come come* her body, oh, her whole body always *whispering*, yes, whispering, back its songs to her, how good it will feel, God, forgive, for I know not what I am

dropping. her fingers, dropping. her limbs, heavy, as bread dough, her fingers, drop, dropping

NO! NO! NO!

inside. yes, God, please INSIDE HER they would go, she knew they would, what to do? And YES! oh God YES! and YES! and it would be over, and she could stretch out, out, on the davenport, and turn, so her fingers could go deeper, in, or maybe lie, down, right here, flat, on the floor *oh God, forgive me for I know not*

it would be all over if she let her fingers

please forgive me for I

the fan, whirring, maybe if I, stick my fingers, in there, instead, I will not stick them down

oh, please, please, someone HELP me

please

whirring, in the background, as if she were dreaming, and already, YES! down, her fingers, YES THEY WERE inside her pants now and she was

crying out, in terror, and fleeing, the front door left open behind her, the porch behind her, the grass, now, the lawn, the sidewalk

SAFE

at last.

The bright sun dazed her eyes. She stood, bewildered, as if she could not remember what she was doing there, why she had come outdoors. Her jeans felt loose. Oh, she had not buttoned them. She did that, feeling suddenly self-conscious, as if all the neighbors were watching her, but she saw no one, only Mr. Bentley out mowing his lawn. She began walking, uncertain where she was going to go.

✿ 20 ✿

She thought about going to the library, but it was closed on Friday afternoons. She thought about going downtown, maybe buying an ice-cream cone or something, but how could she, her money was home and she wasn't about to go back there. She wished for a girl friend to visit, but she had none, not since she and Cheryl stopped running around together. She wandered aimlessly, not knowing what to do. When she found herself standing on the corner by the Methodist church, it seemed somehow as though she'd been heading there all along. She went in.

There was no one inside, of course. The church stood empty most of the week, except for choir practice Wednesday nights, and ladies' aid meetings Thursday afternoons. And it was August. Even Reverend Chettenforth was away this week, he and his wife, on vacation. Marcella remembered when she saw their door closed, the blinds all drawn, the windows down. Everyone was gone. Everybody but the farmers. Even some stores closed, one of the dress shops, and the pool hall.

It was cold inside the main sanctuary, and almost dark, the stained-glass windows filtering the sunlight, throwing patterns, patterns, across the floor.

Marcella liked to come here. It was a good place to be, ever since, oh, especially since she'd come back from camp. This was the first place she'd come, after Colorado. Well, not quite the first place, first home, and change clothes, and eat. Unpack. Try to talk about camp. But the very next day, as soon as she could, she came here, tiptoeing in the side door, climbing the dark stairwell to the sanctuary, pushing through the great double doors—like she'd done today. She had gone to the altar, lit two candles (Reverend Chettenforth wouldn't mind, she had been sure) and she had knelt, praying, "Dear Father in Heaven, help me, please, in this struggle I am about to undertake. I know I am unworthy, oh, Lord, I am not worthy to kiss the hem of your robe, but I will be. Oh, I will be…"

Then she had risen, and taken the big reading Bible, with its huge print, off Reverend Chettenforth's pulpit, and carried it over to the altar table, with its slim white candles, its wine-colored cloth, and its gold-embroidered *holy holy holy*. She laid the Bible on the altar, and she put her right hand over her heart, like when you salute the flag, for she wanted to make it as official as possible, and she placed her left hand on the Holy Word of God Incarnate, raised her eyes to the golden cross, glistening in the candle light, and swore:

"I, Marcella Colby, do solemnly swear to God, in the name of His Son, my Lord and Saviour, Jesus Christ, and in the name of the Holy Ghost, that I will never again, no matter how difficult it is, no matter what I have to do to stop it, I will never, ever, as long as I shall live, by all that is sacred and holy to me, as this Bible is holy, and this cross I gaze upon, I shall never again masturbate."

She had spoken the last word in her tiniest whisper. What an ugly word to say, in a church, of all places, where God must be living at all times, never leaving. She wouldn't have said it, except for taking the oath, wanting to make a promise that would bind her so tightly to Heaven she could never dare break free…oh, and she remembered what she'd done each time she came here, she remembered her oath, and would ask forgiveness for saying that word, here, and thank God for all He'd done for her, asking also His please dear God forgiveness for the awful sins committed in the mountains. And promised, too, never ever again to pretend that she didn't know…because of course, now, she couldn't, for she knew.

She always felt better here, being here strengthened her vow. It was so still. But such a different silence from the silence of the deserted house: calmer, more sanctified. The emptiness seemed to swallow her up, as it had swallowed up the dull thud of her feet on the floor. She shivered a bit. At least it was safe here.

She knelt.

She wanted to pray, but was uncertain how to find her way back, how to find her way back to God, even here, in God's house, uncertain. After this morning, the violence, the dream, what had just happened—how to pray?

"Dear God."

Her voice sounded thin and strained in the huge room.

"It is good to be here."

She couldn't think how to go on. Her legs, bare below her rolled-up jeans, felt very hot against the wooden floor. It was as though she were prostrating herself, not kneeling. That seemed appropriate, somehow.

She lifted her hands *Our Father who art in Heaven,* folding them against her chest *hallowed be the name.* Her words were barely audible: *Thy kingdom come, thy will be done, on earth.* The syllables came out slowly, dragging reluctantly along, *as it is in Heav - en,* sounding like a profound hymn in her head, its words swelling to the final *For thine is the king - dom, and the pow - er, and the glo - ry, for - ev - er. A - men.*

The silence thickened.

It was no good, trying to pray. What she'd done was still too close, how she had almost…How could God believe she was truly sorry, so soon? A curious constraint fell over her. Yet meet. Meet and right so to be here, no question. But not to pray.

She circled the altar railing and climbed the steps, to walk to the pulpit. The Bible was open to Micah, its big print lined up in double columns on each page:

"Therefore I will wail and howl," she read out loud, "I will go stripped and naked: I will make a wailing like the dragons, and mourning as the owls. For her wound is incurable."

Incurable…curable…curable. The word seemed to echo around the empty pews. She turned away.

Round globed bulbs flanked the two-tiered choir loft. Unlit. Wooden chairs neatly folded. A long metal-tipped window opener stood in the corner. Like a haunted house, a church with no people.

Marcella went to the organ, found the key and turned the electricity on. The motor made a low humming sound. The Methodist's organ was enormous, even bigger than the Evangelical's. The keyboards rose in tier after tier, the top row of keys tilted, like seesaws. Marcella shuffled in the bench to find her music. She propped it on the stand, dropped the bench lid, and slid across. Heat made the bench sticky.

Foot pedals lay below, black and white, like an exaggerated piano keyboard. Marcella wiggled her foot around, flexing her ankle. You had to have a loose foot to do the strange heel-toe dance, heel-toe, toe-heel, heel-toe, reaching, stretching, turning the foot back and forth, back and forth, making the notes come smoothly. She pressed a toe tentatively down. *Ba – ROOM* the bass note sounded, huge and somewhat ominous, as it always did in the empty church. *Ba – ROOM.*

How comfortable it all was, how familiar, the toe-heel motions, the special kind of give below the organ keyboard, different from the clatter of a piano, the way you turn your hands while playing, twisting the thumbs and fingers around so there is only a smooth mellow tone, flowing endlessly. She stopped to pull the Band-Aids off. They were bothering her. She slid forward on the bench, to reach a stop. Her jeans tugged against her crotch. She jerked them angrily away.

Pop, pop, she pulled the black pedestaled stops out, here, and here another, and here, this one, and this, her fingers caressing, holding, caressing, her hand turning without even knowing it had paused to turn in midair. She began to play.

O God, our help in a – ges past, Our hope for years to come...

The hymns were nice to warm up on, easier to play than the music Mrs. Robinson had left for her to practice on until fall. She let the notes flow broadly out, a little hesitantly at first, then bringing to life hollow and tremulous tones that waxed stronger, and stronger. Her hands, their fingers bypassing all thought, become the channel for her feeling.

Ho – ly, ho – ly, ho – ly! Lord God Al – might – y!...

She played all four verses, singing as she played, her eyes skipping back and forth between notes and words, the words almost memorized, *ho – ly, ho – ly, ho – ly! though the dark – ness hide Thee,* her singing making the music swell, making her hands spin across the keys as though they were not even material...how glad she was she'd come here. How merciful is the Lord our God in His infinite understanding! Maybe she could even pray, after...

Come, Thou al – might – y King, Help us Thy name to sing.

her hands darting out in midair like hummingbirds, adjusting the stops, pulling here, pushing there, her legs thrusting, and pumping, stretching to their maximum, left, and right, her jeans tugging, but she decided to ignore them, thrusting, stretching, as she sought the high notes, the low notes, *Fa – ther all glor – i – ous, O'er all vic – to – ri – ous* oh! she could play forever this way, she loved it when the music seemed to come of its own accord, pulling her, pushing her, coaxing her to heights she could never attain by will, swirling her way beyond herself, everything seeming to come in extremities, her soul stirring, coming in such extravagances at the climaxes of the songs, receding into the calm, but stirring *A – men,* and on to the next hymn, *Joy – ful, joy – ful we a – dore Thee,* almost without stopping, the notes billowing through the air, playing on, and on, *God of glo – ry, Lord of love; Hearts un – fold like flow'rs be – fore Thee...*

And then it happened.

One minute she was playing *Come, O Lord, like morn – ing sun – light, Mak – ing all life new and free,* and the next moment, oh, no, her jeans tugging hard against her, and she should have stopped, right then, and fixed them, yes, Lord, but she didn't. She kept on playing, instead, *Come, O Lord, like o – cean flood – tides,* and the third, and fourth verses, growing more, and more excited, her thoughts swirling dizzily around her, the music ebbing and flowing, carrying her, transporting her, where, oh, no, the jeans pulling again, but then she was playing, *Praise God, from whom all bless – ings flow, Praise Him, all crea – tures here be – low,* and it was such a short song, she thought she would finish it first, and then, of course, she would have to do something about those jeans, pulling, low, high, tight in against her, she wasn't really doing anything, no, she was not, not like in the house, earlier, when she let her hands drop down, no, she was making them stay right on the keyboard, *Praise Him a – bove, Ye heav – enly host: Praise Fa – ther* it was being done, it was, coming, of its own accord, she wasn't doing, oh, no, anything, oh, no, I should have worn a dress, why wasn't I thinking what I was doing, I should have worn a dress, easier in a dress, oh, no, *Praise Fa – ther, Son, and Ho – ly Ghost,* and it was over, the song, and she, but she mustn't, began again, without even pausing, but her jeans weren't pulling right then, so why fix them, and the music, oh, Lord, in her, yes, Lord, all around her, *Praise God,* not her, doing it, but whatever it was, doing it

One moment she was playing *from whom* and the next *from whom all* moment it was as though her body *bless – ings* had taken over herself, oh, no, *bless – ings flow flow flow FLOW FLOW FLOW* as though, oh, no, her body was moving her, *Praise Him, all crea – tures* and she was rubbing, rubbing, *here be – low* right in the middle of the doxology, rubbing in movements of wildest abandonment and friction against the organ bench, BE – LOOOOOOOOOOOOOOOWWWWW, causing her hands to fly off the keys, so only the bass note, held out, in the church, OOOOOOOOOOOOOOOOOWWWWWWW causing her hands to fly off, and down, and oh, NO!

so sudden, so piercing, that anyone listening would have heard only the last thud of the pedal, letting go. And then, silence. Silence. Silence.

Oh yes, Lord, oh yes, oh Lord, oh yes, our help in ages past, joyful, joyful, oh Lord, yes, Lord, yes, I did take the vow, yes Lord, I did take and I did Eat, Lord, I did EAT, Lord, oh, yes, I did, I did, but the snake, He made me, yes, oh, God, and in the church, too, in the sanctuary, how could I, my good Lord Jesus Christ Saviour of all Mankind, how could I, my good Lord, right on the organ bench, right next to the altar, right in the midst of, midst of, midst of, midst of, PLENTY, Lord, oh yes, PLENTY you have given me to eat, oh yes, but

but,

but it was not enough, oh, no, Lord, not enough, not nearly enough for this Thy wicked child laid here before you, laid here low before you, see, see, Lord how her head hangs off the organ bench, oh, how she weeps, how she weeps, like a dragon wails, Lord, like an owl mourns, oh, so deep is her sorrow, deep, Lord, that the snake did tempt her, and she did eat.

Our Father Who Art in Heaven, Hallowed be Thy Name, Thy Kingdom Come Come Come Come Come Come

see how I prostrate myself before Thee, Lord, oh, how I prostrate myself. low, low, low, I hang my head oh my God, I am not worthy to touch the hem of your robe, nay, unworthy am I to eat the dust shaken from your heels, did eat, oh, Lord, yes, I admit it. I admit it. See, here, Lord, look, I admit it, this is what I did, I did, I did, I did hear the snake and He did tempt me, "take down your clothes, Marcella," and yes, oh Lord, yes, and I did, yes, and my body lies stripped and exposed before you, the first time I did it, it was the snake, that tempted, now, oh, Lord, it is me, with my fingers, naked, spread upon the bench for all to see, oh Lord, yes Lord, you can see as well as I yes Lord, my disgrace. I did not turn away from the temptation that You sent to me, I am not worthy to eat the dust, and then the snake said, take, eat, this is your body, prepared for you, take, eat, and I knew, Lord, I knew, oh Lord, what unholy things he did suggest, oh, yes, Lord, knew, and I

my God, what have I done?

took my fingers and I did poke, oh Lord, poke, yes Lord like this, here, right here, I take my finger and I do

what are you doing?

poke it up here like this oh Lord, my God, it feels so good, so incredibly GOOD my Lord god, it does, oh, yes, that is what she did say, and is saying now, yes, Lord

again? doing it again? oh NO!

do poke it IN. Aaaaaaaahhhh, Lord, and IN, Lord, and yes, yes, I am doing it again, one more time, Lord, see and in, and no, and in, and yes, and have to (excuse me, Lord) push my buttocks up high in the air to

oh, no, what if someone sees you?

to come, oh, Lord, kingdom come, oh Lord, let your blessed kingdom come here *on earth,* Lord, yes, COME, and I am COMING, Lord, I am COMING, oh God Almighty From Whom All Blessings Flow, and oh, yes, Lord, did eat, once, now twice, yes, Lord, yes, and He your only begotten Son, He went into the desert, yes, Lord, and the Devil did tempt Him, and He did hold Himself against the Devil, yes, Lord, He did, for He was tempted and did not eat, did not, oh Lord, but Marcella, aaaaaahhhh. Marcella, aaaaaaaahhh, she did gobble, gobble, gobble, gobble, yes, and does, and did, gobble, gobble, into the kitchen, UP the soda bottle, into the bathroom, yes, UP the ice cube, OVER the bathtub rim, OVER the pillow, UP the soda, oh, Lord, there is nothing she would not try, UP fingers, ice cubes, washcloths, what next, letter openers, scissors, butcher knives, oh dear God Lord there is nothing that I wouldn't try

and sweating. oh, no, all over the organ bench. oh, no.

no good in her. Ha, Lord, look, no good, none at all, ha, Lord, what were we pretending about, in the morning, in the sunlight, in the Garden with you, ha, ha, that I might be a Christian, ho, ho, a missionary even, spreading your Holy Word in foreign lands, who were you kidding, God, there is no good in her.

get up, you fool, what if someone sees you

none. none at all, you think that was bad, oh Lord, yes, evil, what is happening to me I cannot seem to control it, it is, my legs, like dough, it is, oh, dear God, black, all around, like in a dream, and they are COMING, Lord, yes, oh, they are COMING, all white, and light, in through the door and down through that big tent of a ceiling, COMING to gather me home, see, me, Lord, how they take me, oh, God, how they take me off the organ bench, oh, yes, God, I am Yours, forever and ever amen, and never to sin again, oh, no, never I swear, I take the vow, oh, I LIGHT THE CANDLES LORD, and how they are taking me, yes, prostrate, Lord, I go prostrate, with my jeans hanging down around my ankles and your carpet, Lord, your holy holy holy green carpet, Lord, see how it scratches, its hard and sticky tufts grasping at my knees, my thighs, oh, yes, oh Lord, how it scratches like a thousand tiny fingers my belly, Lord, oh, yes, my legs, raw, yes, raw, in me, no good

not again. oh, no Marcella, please not again. You have got to stop this, you've got to STOP

trying to stop me, Lord, oh, no, because we know, don't we, into the desert, oh, yes, Lord, crawling along the terrible hot and turbulent desert of temptation all the way to the altar Lord, yes, God, prostrate before your Holy Altar, yes, on my face, yes, my face down, don't worry, Marcella, the railing will hide you, no one can see you there, oh, Lord, yes, down, for I always likes to do it best with my face down, and under the pillow, yes, and no pillow here, but that's okay, Lord, that's okay, we aren't choosy, we do it anywhere, anytime, any place, oh, yes, Lord, and I can always pull my pants up if I hear someone coming, I am not dumb, Lord, if the outside door creaks, or the stairs, there will be time, Lord, and time, yes, and see how I raise myself oh Lord, yes, and see how these *snakes,* how these *snakes* of mine, see how they reach up, Lord, oh yes, Lord, how they do TAKE,

Lord, your holy white candles, yes Lord, oh, yes, how they do take your candles off your altar, and they do, oh, yes, Lord, there is no good, no good in me anywhere, and they take, eat, this is my body which is broken for you, dear God, take, eat, and they, yes, candles, yes, into the ho – ly place, yes, into the passage, yes, that's what they say, yes, Lord, oh God most high stop me if you will, and there, and there, and see how my snakes push the candles UP Lord, they are COMING to take me

perverted, oh! dear God please forgive, forgive, forgive for I know not what

Oh, Lord, God, giver and taker of all good things, He that giveth life, taketh away life, yes, Lord, away, and before your Holy Altar, Lord, yes, Lord, where did she take the vow, I, Marcella Colby, and bear with me, Lord, it takes a while the third time, and the white candles, oh, yes, Lord, and the red, oh yes, no black, no more, and the white, flash red, flash white, flash Lord and

MY GOD! WHAT ARE YOU DOING!

and yes, UP, yes UP yes UP this is my body yes UP and take EAT and yes UP and this is my blood YES EAT UP which was shed for thee UP UP UP, shed, and oh yes, Lord, the candle, yes, and the

arms off. I've got to cut the arms off. Not the fingers, fingers not enough, oh, no, not, stumps of hands in, yes, red, white, blood of lamb, UP they go, and cut the arms off, and the elbows in, oh, no, they cannot reach and then SAFE SAFE I'd be, and only candles, and ice picks, and butcher knives, and

no, no, not enough, not enough, got to get it OUT of there, OUT OUT that is the only way, the arms, the hands, the fingers, only snakes, not the sin, oh, the sin, so ripe and rotten in the belly of Eve yes must GO

OUT

but where. how, oh Lord, and the third time she rose from the dead and she

but how, oh Lord, where, oh, help me

it is nothing. it is only the third coming, and the fourth, and the fifth, and sixth, and seventh, yea, even unto forever, coming, forever and ever, coming, cannot stop, cannot make it stop doing it, must get rid, somehow, cut it out

if your eye offend thee

OUT OUT OUT

better eyeless than burn in hellfire

OUT

She pulled her pants up, but took the candle out, first, and wiped it on her pants, and put it back upon the altar. Then she pulled her pants up, but did not fasten them, because of what remained. To be done. Yes, Lord.

and went

downstairs.

down the stairwell, oh, Lord, yes, I am yours, and yes, God, this is my body, this is my blood, ha, Lord, and where is the lamb that lovest thee, thorns, next, Lord, yes, and of course, knives are in the kitchen, where else? and down the stairwell, yes, and across the big basement room, yes, no one there, now, no one coming, no one to see her, no, not here, as quiet as upstairs, and only the sound of her feet soft on the floor, yes, Lord, and the groaning, which had, yes, oh, begun, yes, when she started down, oh Lord.

oh, come, come, come, come, come to the church in the wild wood, oh, come to the church in the glen glen glen

it was getting black again, like in her dream, black, and she fought to keep herself in, somehow, yes, focused, so that she could find the knives, and holding her pants up with one hand, so that when she did find them, she wouldn't even have to unzip her pants, but just open them, and begin

again. begin, again, day after day after futile day, she could not begin, again, not this way, where do they keep them? and opening up one drawer after another, and the black, moving in, could she, yes, could she hold it off long enough to

and found it, then. them. long and lean and steel and one sharp edge, yes, and a point, oh, yes, and letting her pants fall open so she could feel them with her thumb, yes, the edges, with her fingers, with her thumbs, to find the sharpest one, and yes, selecting, picking it, up, huge, long, steel blade, black handle, knife, then, and laughing

oh how had she *come* to this place

laughing, she began to

draw the blade, yes, Lord, once across her tongue, yes, dear God, for all the lies told, yes, but oh, it didn't even draw blood, she couldn't taste a thing, razors better, swifter, cleaner, never mind. plenty of time, later, after you

OH, MY GOD!

never mind. it won't hurt much, just a bit at first and

NO! PLEASE NO!

then she began to

draw the blade across

her stomach, yes, there, across the belly of Eve, and then, yes, down, yes down and

oh, no, please help me

down and down and down and

now

the tip low, parting the pubic hair

shove

and black, like in a dream, black, red, black, and then, shoving, and then shoving, and then shoving, and then Oh God our help in Ages Past shoving, shove, shove, shove, yes, yes, yes, yes, yes yes

But it wouldn't penetrate. Not the blade. Not through skin. She tried, but the knife blade was dull, so dull, it would not puncture skin, not even the point was sharp enough, they were all dull, it wasn't her fault, she had picked the sharpest one, and tried. Yes, tried. But couldn't even

OH MY GOD! MARCELLA! WHAT ARE YOU DOING...

the knife blade, cool, so cool against her skin, so deliciously cool...but how curiously tough, skin, how tough. Easy enough this morning, cutting herself before she even knew, but now. She tried again. Pushed. And pushed, but the skin would not give way, and she didn't have the heart, she didn't have the heart, to pick the knife up and lunge it at herself, plunge it through, it would all be over so fast that way, but she couldn't...a little at a time, yes, try again, once more, a bit here, some there. Mutilated. She could even, yes, that's it, she must, cut herself, down THERE, cut her LIPS off, slice them through, clean, like the belly of a fish, yes, and then, maybe, she would not want to put her fingers, dip them, in no! Ow, never, no...but maybe if she really broke skin, they would stitch her up, tight, closed, so she couldn't, get in

what are you doing here. what do you think you're doing.

the kitchen, snapping suddenly back into focus. The wooden drawer still hanging, green and white, open. The knife still in her hand, the knife, her hand gripping its black handle. The skin, its soft covering of curly hair. The skin, indented under the knife blade. The skin, bending in, in, in, in

Oh! What are you

No! No! Seeing it...

Oh, no! I could kill myself that way
and throwing the knife down. Oh, no, no, no, no

It seemed an eternity before Marcella heard the knife hit the floor. She was shaking all over and she could even hear a scream building, way at the back of her head. Gathering. But she shook her head. The scream went away.

She couldn't stop trembling. She stood there, shaking and shaking, hugging herself and quivering, until she heard herself saying, "Stop it. Just stop it."

She was still, amazingly, alive. She had done what she had done, upstairs, in the sanctuary, sacrilege beyond her wildest imaginings, and still she lived. She had come down here to do her worst, to commit the ultimate sin against God, to, yes, admit it, to defy Him—to stab herself, to mutilate, maybe even kill, and still. Still she was, astoundingly, alive.

When the trembling seemed to have departed altogether, she picked up the knife, pulled open the kitchen drawer once more, and returned it. It was so dull—she felt the blade gingerly before she dropped it in—so dull, no wonder it couldn't break skin. Maybe there was another, sharper one. She looked in. The horror dropped back over her; she clutched the edge of the drawer with both hands, squeezing it until her knuckles turned white. "Oh, no, oh, no, oh NO!" she said, her voice rude and loud in the church silence. She felt the scream rising again—but before she had to stifle it, it melted away by itself.

She stopped crying, then, and wiped her drying tears off her cheek with the back of her hand. She felt all weak inside, like a huge balloon in her chest had burst, leaving everything limp. She looked around. So quiet down here. And musty, like basements always are.

She zipped her pants. No need to stay. Not any more. It was finished. She turned and walked, heels sounding, across the empty room, up the narrow staircase, and out of the black cave of the church. The sudden rush of heat made the air seem thick. She squinted against the glare of the August sun. Dozens of rays rose, shimmering, from the pavement. Somewhere, grasshoppers hummed. Summers were always like this.

Her head began to clear, as though her ears had popped—hurting, but setting something free. A dried strand of hair tugged at the skin of her cheek. She pulled it loose. She could never return. There was only…She headed across the churchyard. Whatever there was, she had already begun.

About the Author

A best-selling, national prize-winning, internationally published author of poetry and prose, Marilyn Coffey has composed six hundred poems, dozens of prose pieces, and four books, many set in the Great Plains states of Kansas and Nebraska. Her work has appeared in Australia, Canada, Denmark, England, India, and Japan.

Her novel, Marcella, is a groundbreaker: the first novel written in English to use female masturbation as a main theme. Coffey's biography, Mail-Order Kid: An Orphan Train Rider's Story, is an Amazon and Kindle best seller. Her poem, "Pricksong," won a national Pushcart Prize. Her memoir, Great Plains Patchwork, was excerpted in Atlantic Monthly (cover story), Natural History and by 15 book publishers.

Known as a prose stylist, Coffey received a Master Alumnus award for distinction in the field of writing from the University of Nebraska. The university's library collects her papers.

A trained journalist (B.A., University of Nebraska, 1959) and creative writer (M.F.A., Brooklyn College, 1981), Coffey is also an interpretive reader who has appeared before 130 groups in twelve states, from Maine to Texas.

Now retired, Coffey taught writing at Boston University, Pratt Institute in Brooklyn, and Fort Hays State University in Kansas for thirty-four years, twice earning tenure.

www.mail-orderkid.com   www.marilyncoffey.net